YOU'RE
MY
KIND

by Clare Lydon

custard
books

First Edition March 2019
Published by Custard Books
Copyright © 2019 Clare Lydon
ISBN: 978-1-912019-91-5

Cover Design: Rachel Lawston
Editor: Cheyenne Blue
Typesetting: Adrian McLaughlin

Find out more at: www.clarelydon.co.uk
Follow me on Twitter: @clarelydon
Follow me on Instagram: @clarefic

Also by Clare Lydon

Other Novels
The Long Weekend
Nothing To Lose: A Lesbian Romance
Twice In A Lifetime
Once Upon A Princess

London Romance Series
London Calling (Book 1)
This London Love (Book 2)
A Girl Called London (Book 3)
The London Of Us (Book 4)
London, Actually (Book 5)
Made In London (Book 6)

All I Want Series
All I Want For Christmas (Book 1)
All I Want For Valentine's (Book 2)
All I Want For Spring (Book 3)
All I Want For Summer (Book 4)
All I Want For Autumn (Book 5)
All I Want Forever (Book 6)

Boxsets
All I Want Series Boxset, Books 1-3
All I Want Series Boxset, Books 4-6
All I Want Series Boxset, Books 1-6
London Romance Series Boxset, Books 1-3

Acknowledgements

This book has been a long time in the making. I first began to write it in May last year, after the kernel of an idea formed in my mind. But then, after committing 15k words to the page over one weekend, I left the project hanging. However, I was drawn back to it at the end of 2018. Once I started over, there was no stopping the story tumbling out.

The inspiration for the baking school came from the wonderful Fair Cake in Greenwich. Thanks so much to the fabulous owner Shikhita Singh who let me sit in on the classes and told me how and why she set up her cake school. She even baked me the best cake I've ever tasted. I can now officially say that Swiss meringue buttercream truly is da bomb. Thanks also to my friend Rachel Batchelor, property developer extraordinaire. Thanks for telling me the ins and outs of property auctions, as well as the amount of times you visit Wickes in an average week. Answer: a lot.

Thanks also to my trusted first reader, HP Munro, for your initial feedback that helped elevate this book to the next level. Buckets of gratitude to my ARC team manager

Tammara Adams, and all my early readers who caught the last-minute errors that made this book the best it could possibly be.

Design plaudits to Rachel Lawston for the cake-a-licious cover. I absolutely love it. A bunch of thanks to Cheyenne Blue for her considered editing skills. This is the first full project we've worked on, but it won't be the last. Also, a tip of the nib to Adrian McLaughlin for his cheerleading and typesetting prowess. The prettiness you hold in your hands is all down to him.

No book of mine would be complete without saying huge thanks to my wife Yvonne for always being there for me. Without her encouragement and reassurance that my writing doesn't suck, I wouldn't get through any book project. Quite simply, she's my rock. I love you, darling.

Last but definitely not least, thanks to you for buying this book and supporting my work. Without you, I wouldn't be doing my dream job, so I can't thank you enough. I hope you enjoy this book, because I wrote it especially for you.

If you fancy getting in touch, you can do so using one of the methods below — I'm most active on Twitter, Facebook or Instagram.

Twitter: @ClareLydon
Facebook: www.facebook.com/clare.lydon
Instagram: @clarefic
Find out more at: www.clarelydon.co.uk
Contact: mail@clarelydon.co.uk

Thank you so much for reading!

For Marc Evans.
Forever missed.

Chapter One

I was wearing the wrong shoes. My new navy brogues were rubbing already, and I'd only walked to the bloody car. But today, they were the least of my worries.

"Okay, we can do this. We can *totally* do this." Gemma reached across and put her hand on mine, her short, pristine nails freshly painted dark red. "You're going to be fine. I know it's a big day, and Kerry dropped a bomb last night telling us you-know-who was coming too, but today is not about her; it's about James and Kerry. Got it?"

I gave Gemma a tight-lipped smile. I was scared I'd contradict her if I opened my mouth.

Outside, the May morning was in full swing, sunshine dripping off the car even though it was only 9:30 am. It reminded me of those endless summer days we used to share at university. The end of term, exams done and worries shed. Us slathering layers of coconut oil on our skin and basting ourselves before we knew any better. With my fair hair and pale skin, the sun always won that battle. Even the grass outside reminded me of our university grounds, cut to regulation length, neat and ordered. Everything as it should be.

The complete opposite of this morning, in fact. Because today, we were burying James. The first of the gang to die.

"I'm trying to distract myself, but my mind keeps pinballing from one disaster to another. James, Maddie, James, Maddie." I put my hands to my face. If Maddie turned up with a beautiful wife, I was going to dissolve on the spot. "I need a drink and it's not even ten. Have I mentioned this is a stupid time for a funeral?"

Gemma patted my knee as I dropped my hands. "Only about 47 times on the way over here." My best friend gave me a look, before patting her short, dark hair. She'd had it cut short this week and she was still getting used to it. Everyone at work kept telling her she looked like Halle Berry in that James Bond film. Gemma said they needed to update their references, but I'd told her to concentrate on the 'you look like a Bond girl' part.

"Repeat after me. My name is Justine Thomas, I'm a successful entrepreneur and a gorgeous woman to boot." Gemma waited a few seconds. "You're meant to repeat it."

"I'm not five years old."

"No," she agreed. "But you're about to meet the woman who completely shattered your heart, so I imagine right now you feel about 24 years old. I just want to remind you that in the intervening years since Maddie, you've flourished, opened a successful business and been featured in national newspapers because of it. You're a big deal."

I laughed. "I'm not a fucking big deal. Maddie's probably a millionaire by now, you know what she was like. Driven. Determined. High-achiever."

"And what are you? You're all those things and more, and lovely into the bargain." She tapped the mirror on my sun visor. "Take a look in the mirror, see for yourself."

I sighed. "I know I've done okay."

"You just need to be reminded, what with Maddie looming."

"She's not looming. And she was a very long time ago."

"I know, but it still happened and has shaped your life ever since."

I creased my face, before turning to Gemma. Not only my best friend, but also my business partner for the past five years. "I appreciate your concern, but I can cope. I'm an adult now, fully grown, responsible even. Maddie and I were a decade ago. Today, I'll be civil, we'll smile, and then I never have to see her again. I knew this might happen one day, and James has brought that day forward. Bloody James, going and dying on us." I smiled, even though every time I said it, my heart broke a little bit more.

I'd loved James like a brother. Plus, he was far less annoying than my *actual* brother. A wave of sadness washed down me, and I reminded myself: Maddie wasn't important today. James and Kerry were.

Cars were beginning to pull up around us, and brightly dressed mourners walked past. One man wore a Union Jack three-piece suit. He'd clearly got Kerry's message about no black. One of our best friends was about to bury a man she'd loved for 13 years. I couldn't even fathom how she must be feeling.

I cleared my throat. "Should we make a move?" I took a deep breath. "I want to be there when Kerry arrives with her parents. She's going to need our support."

Gemma nodded. "Course." She pulled down her sun visor, got her lipstick out of her bag and applied more colour. "How do I look?"

She'd told me earlier the lipstick was called Brave, which seemed apt. It popped against her soft, brown skin. Gemma had that knack of looking incredible whatever she was wearing. Today, what she was wearing was certainly a statement.

I appraised her yellow trousers and orange shirt, which she'd combined with white patent shoes. "How do you look? Like you're the entertainment for a kids' birthday party."

She laughed. "That's just the look I was going for."

A knock on the window interrupted us. It was our friend, Rob, in a sombre black suit and tie. He looked like he was going to a funeral, exactly what Kerry had instructed us not to wear. Gemma rolled down the window.

"All right, cake ladies! You coming in, or planning on sitting in a hot tin box for the rest of the morning?" Rob gave us a broad grin. "I hear there's air-con inside, so I'd plump for that if I were you."

"Very droll," Gemma replied. "We were just getting out. Where's Jeremy?"

He grimaced. "Babysitter fell through, so he's not here. He dropped me off in town just now. He's devastated, but sends his love."

I pouted. I loved Rob and his husband Jeremy, but since they'd spawned twins last year via surrogacy, it was pretty common for only one of them to turn up to occasions. However, Rob was a regular fixture in our lives, as he ran the bakery opposite our cake school in Bristol. We were business neighbours as well as friends.

"And what's with the black?"

He shrugged. "I had a way jauntier outfit on, but then the twins puked on me three times. Each. In the end, this was almost my only item of clean clothing that was ironed."

"Rob!" someone yelled from across the car park. He looked up and waved as someone I didn't know walked up and gave him a hug. This was the first funeral I'd ever been to, and it was already striking me that it was like any big life occasion, only without the guest of honour.

I glanced at Gemma. "Shall we?" I opened the door and just as my brogues hit the tarmac, a brand-new red Mini pulled up beside us. It had tinted windows and those go-faster hub caps. Total boy-racer territory. Whoever was driving this car clearly wanted the world to know who they were.

The Mini's engine shut off as I slammed the passenger door of Gemma's Ford Focus. I reached my arms above my head, performing a full-body stretch. It had only been a 20-minute journey to the crematorium, but I was already sticky from the heat. I was glad I'd opted for pale blue trousers paired with a short-sleeved printed shirt and no jacket.

I threw a smile across the top of the car to Gemma and Rob, but they were both looking at me with panic etched on their faces. What was going on?

A car door slammed behind me, and my two friends froze.

Suddenly, I knew who that Mini belonged to, who it was who wanted to get noticed. Who it was standing behind me, causing my friends to turn into ice statues even on a blazing hot day.

I closed my eyes, my heart slamming into my ribs, all the hairs on my neck standing up one by one, craning their necks to get a better look.

The number of times I'd thought about this moment over the years, and now it was about to happen.

I clenched my fists at my sides, the itch of anxiety burning my throat. I took a deep breath and spun round. And there was Maddie. The ex that counted. Still tall and slim. Still beautiful. Still with the most styled, thick eyebrows I'd ever encountered. And how were her blonde waves still so goddamn shiny and perfect?

Just like that, and exactly as Gemma had predicted, I was 24 again. Lost, abandoned, heart-broken. Only now, coming over my emotional hill at speed were the dual cavalries of anger and rage.

I'd wondered how I was going to react, and now I was getting my answer.

Yep, I was completely over it.

Maddie was dressed in fitted black trousers, black shirt and black lace-ups. She hadn't got the memo about no black. I was inordinately pleased. It showed that, even if she tried to wheedle her way back in, she wasn't part of the gang anymore. That was important. She'd lost the right a long time ago.

"Hi, Justine." She held me with her piercing grey eyes, and my heart stuttered. "It's good to see you."

Maddie Kind. Once the author of my dreams, then the author of my nightmares.

I couldn't say the same.

Chapter Two

We met at university, all of us raring to go. Out of our parental homes and into our halls of residence like we were starring in some cool TV show. At least, that's what our first taste of freedom felt like. We were invincible, like anything could happen. Because when you're 18, that's what life feels like: scary, incredible, wonky.

It all seemed so long ago now. I avoided Maddie's intense stare and tried to radiate confidence and calm. I was anything but. Seeing her again brought up so many memories, most of them bad. Most of them from after *us*. I still wanted answers, but now wasn't the time.

Plus, my bladder needed emptying. I indicated with my head towards the main crematorium as Gemma landed at my side, Rob at the other.

Reinforcements had finally arrived.

"I have to go to the loo." Not the first line I'd imagined I'd utter to my ex, but then, real life never mimicked what happened in your head, did it?

I walked past a group of men in black suits, already wiping the sweat from the back of their necks. James had died at the start of the summer. Today was the sort of day we'd all have met at a pub by the river for lunch and drinks. Stories of our former life coating the air like melted honey. Raucous laughter from James. He'd always been the loudest. The one who made people turn their heads. He was still doing it today, wasn't he?

The toilet signs were polished brass with the black outline of a woman in a ridiculously uniform A-line skirt. A bit like the ones we'd been tasked to create in sewing class in school. I'd made a bright orange version, the colour of burnt sunsets. My teacher, a kind Australian woman who was probably around the age I am now, had made encouraging noises from the sidelines, while probably wondering where the hell I was going to wear such a thing. It was a fair question. Who knew where that skirt was now?

Once inside the loo, I took some deep breaths. Today was going to be long. I might even cry. I had tissues in my bag, just in case. Kerry had told us she wanted floods of tears, gales of laughter, and rivers of snot rolling down the crematorium aisles. Did crematoriums have aisles? I wasn't sure.

The only issue was, I hadn't shed a single tear since Maddie left. Then, I'd cried for weeks. But since then? A whole decade of nothing.

Perhaps James's funeral was the place to change that.

Whatever, I knew I had to stop hiding in the toilet. James would have told me that Maddie's presence today didn't change anything I'd achieved in the intervening years. I was still a strong woman. I still ran a successful cake school. James would tell me to go out there and be the strong person I am. Because it had only been five minutes since Maddie walked back into my life, and I could already feel my skin tingling with nerves, could already hear my confidence scuttling out the door.

I wasn't going to let Maddie railroad me. I could do this. How many hours had I spent conjuring words to Maddie in my head, telling her exactly what I thought of her? Numerous train journeys, hundreds of bus rides, thousands of steps on endless pavements. But now my chance to tell her was here, ten years later, it was all a little... stale. A little after-the-fact.

Seeing Maddie and knowing what had happened between us, my body had reacted like always. But I didn't trust my body: it was just a collection of muscles and veins, after all.

It was my mind I trusted, my mind I could control. And my mind was telling my body to calm the fuck down, get back out there and do what James would have wanted me to do.

"Woman up, Justine!" That had been James's catchphrase. When it came to being a feminist ally, James was at the head of the pack. All of which made it that little more bitter it was James who'd died.

Back out in the glaring sunshine, I clocked Gemma waving at me. Maddie was standing to the side, chatting to Daniel, who'd lived in our halls at university. Daniel had always had a bottle of Southern Comfort in his room back then, in case he was invited to an impromptu party. Nobody had liked Daniel, and yet, here he was at James's funeral. I bet he had a bottle of Southern Comfort in his muted grey backpack. Who brought a backpack to a funeral? Was he going hiking afterwards?

I walked over to Gemma as Rob approached, putting an arm around her. Gemma put her head on Rob's shoulder, leaning in.

"What a fucking day. Can't believe I'm in a suit. James would have wanted us all in shorts, wouldn't he?" Rob tugged at his black tie. It was only when I looked closer, I saw it had tiny reindeer stamped all over it.

I pulled it out from his chest and raised a single eyebrow.

He slapped my hand away and smoothed it back down. "It's my nod to the party theme." He rubbed his hand around the back of his neck and did a sweep of the crowd, which had swelled considerably since we arrived.

"Have you spoken to her yet?" Rob leaned his head in the direction of Maddie.

I shook my head. "Not really. But when I do, I'm sure it'll be fine." Lies, all lies.

I glanced over at Maddie, who was nodding intently at Daniel. I lowered my gaze to her left hand. No rings. And then I mentally slapped myself.

For fuck's sake, Justine, it doesn't matter whether she's got a ring or not.

My thoughts were interrupted as the funeral cortege crept up the pristine tarmac. It stopped in front of the thick wooden main doors, now flung open. A polished mahogany box glinted through the glass, but none of it seemed real. I was still waiting for James to amble across the car park, telling us it was all a big joke. Imploring us to get down the pub, make his a pint, and none of that poncey expensive stuff, either.

Maddie's laughter split the air just as Kerry got out of the car, and everybody nearby turned to glare at her. Maddie's cheeks turned puce.

I looked towards the coffin, and to Kerry. Her face pensive, her dress lemon yellow, her fair curly hair falling all around her face. So far, she was holding it together.

Emotion swelled in me. Maybe I would cry today. If anybody deserved it, it was James.

Chapter Three

The wake was being held in a nearby rugby club, and as Gemma swung her car into the crowded car park, she swerved to avoid two other funeral guests, missing them by a whisker. When she cut the engine, she let out a noisy breath that told me it'd been a little too close for comfort.

"Fuck me. Killing two of the funeral guests might have been a bit hard to explain."

Inside, the space reminded me of the many sports club bars we'd visited when we played hockey at university. This one had worn-in carpets and far too much pine, but the saving grace was the gallons of light let in by the large windows which overlooked the playing fields beyond. Even better, outside was a deck scattered with picnic tables, and the patio doors were thrown open, inviting people onto it. Just before the bar, a buffet was already laid out, featuring sandwiches, pork pies, cake and crisps. Funerals and carb comas went hand in hand.

An arm around my shoulder squeezed tight, and I turned to see Gemma, with Maddie walking up behind. Maddie had come to the funeral on her own, which was brave. Just like Gemma's lipstick.

Seeing her again, my heart suffered a mini-tremor. I still wasn't used to her being this close.

"Drink?" It was a rhetorical question. I turned, walking to the crowded bar and ordered a large white wine without pausing for breath. I didn't even care it was Stowells. Any port in a storm.

When I turned to get Gemma's order, I was grateful Maddie hadn't followed. "I wish I could just focus on James and not her." Easier said than done. "You want a cider?"

Gemma nodded, rubbing the small of my back. "Please." She paused. "And you can focus on James — just decide to. Plus, Maddie doesn't look like she's here to cause trouble."

"She never does though, does she?"

Rob arrived at my side. "Pint of Peroni, pretty please, favourite friend." His tie was already off, his jacket discarded.

"Where were you? We waited and then were told you'd got another lift from the crematorium."

Rob looked down at the ground, wincing as he brought his eyes level with mine. "Don't shout at me, but I got a lift with Maddie. She didn't know where the rugby club was, so I offered. We can't ignore her all day, can we?"

I creased my brow. "I'm going to try."

"How was the drive?" Gemma took her cider from the bar.

Rob paused before replying. "It was fine. Illuminating." I bet. "How so?"

He picked up his pint and we followed him to a table near the patio doors before he continued. "She seemed lovely and genuinely contrite for what happened in the past. Plus, she's having a tough time at the moment with family issues." He held up her hand. "And yes, before you start talking about karma turning up and biting her on the arse, I know she deserves it." He cocked his head. "But, I dunno, it's been a long time, hasn't it? Water under the bridge and all that."

"Not enough water yet for me." Maddie might be a scientist heading up a treatment centre for breast cancer. She might be hailed in many quarters for her good deeds. She might be a philanthropist of the highest order. It didn't make any difference to what had happened and the way I felt.

Rob shut up.

Gemma put a hand on my arm. "We're on your side, remember? Team Justine all the way." Then she punched the air like she was in a John Hughes film.

"We're not at university anymore," I countered, enjoying her show of solidarity nonetheless.

"We're always at university," she replied.

Rob nodded, holding up his pint. "Team Justine too, natch."

I smiled. I could always rely on my oldest and dearest friends. "Thanks. It's just taking some getting used to, her being back. Today isn't what I expected."

Rob shrugged. "We're at James's funeral. Sometimes life isn't what you expect."

A chair being pulled back made us all look up.

And there was my past, standing in front of me again. All 5ft 10 of her. Her jaw was still square and strong; newsreader reliable. She still had that same golden skin that travelled for miles across her body like the Sahara Desert. Plus, her eyes still shone that weird soft grey, with flecks of gold.

No, sometimes life wasn't what you expected.

"Mind if I sit?" Maddie's gaze jumped hesitantly between Gemma and I, while she gave Rob a smile.

Rob was already an ally for Maddie. *Traitor.*

Gemma held out a hand. "Of course."

Jesus, her too?

And then Kerry was beside us. "Gem, can you come and give me a hand with the cake? James left specific instructions and if you're there, the cake-maker, it's far less likely I'll drop it." She paused. "Actually, could you come too, Rob, just in case we need brawn as well as brains?"

I wanted to scream "Not now Kerry!", but it was her husband's funeral, so that wasn't allowed. Instead, Gemma threw me an apologetic glance and Rob followed.

And then it was just Maddie and I. She had a few more wrinkles, but not even one grey hair. She'd aged beautifully, because that's how Maddie did life.

* * *

"How are you?" Maddie pulled her shoulders back, and her gaze skittered around my face, never quite meeting my eye. She wasn't brave enough yet. Instead, she ran her index finger up and down her bottle of San Miguel, and smiled as two elderly ladies swayed past the table, one of their ample bottoms banging against the wood.

How was I? I was trying to ignore the pace of my heartbeat, the rush of blood currently flooding my cheeks.

"I'm good." I dragged my gaze to meet hers. Then I held it firm. "It's been quite some time." That was the understatement of the year.

"It has." She nodded at her own statement, sucking on her top lip, a habit I remembered from old. Just like that, I got a flashback to our final year at uni in Bath, when Maddie had worn the same concentrated look all through her finals. The same look that told me she thought she was going to fuck up. She hadn't. She'd got a first.

"James told me you're a bigwig in cakes these days, which I have to say, was a surprise."

Just when had James had time to do that? "From beyond the grave?"

She smiled. That hadn't changed: her smile was still electric. You could use it to power a room and still have sparkle left over. I pushed down a wobble and tightened every muscle I had. With Maddie, I needed a strong core.

"We met up for lunch a few times. Occasional beers after work. He kept me up to date on everything."

This was news. "He never said."

Maddie gave me a sad smile. "You know James."

Evidently not.

She flicked her gaze to me, then looked away abruptly.

I did the same. Outside, a woman in a yellow top was laughing at something her friend had said.

Sitting here with Maddie, my capacity to laugh had completely disappeared.

I looked around. Kerry and Gemma were fussing over the buffet, clearing a space for James's massive cake in the shape of a rocket. It had been his dying wish, so Kerry had honoured it and Gemma had made it. James had said you get a special cake for a wedding, but nothing for a funeral. They didn't look like they were going to rush back and save me anytime soon.

I ground my teeth together, searching for something to say, but my mind was blank.

"Still living near Bath?" Maddie asked.

I took another slug of wine. "Just outside. I've got a little house in one of the villages."

"So we're not living that far apart," she said. "I'm doing up a flat in the city centre."

A stab to my gut, then the knife twisted a little more. "You live in Bath?" Last I heard Maddie was living in London. London I could cope with. London was far enough away. But Bath? That was my manor. But what had I expected? That Maddie would observe a no-travel zone?

She nodded. "Sort of. Moved back about six months ago. I'm a property developer and there are a lot of opportunities here. I lived in London and Spain for a while, but I always had a soft spot for Bath when we lived there in our uni days, so I decided, why not? I'm mostly living in Bristol at Mum's old house, but crashing in the Bath flat when I need to."

There was me thinking I was safe, but no. Bath wasn't a big city; while Bristol was where I worked, and only a handful of miles away. We were bound to run into each other sooner or later.

She sat back. "I'm not doing this to make you feel uncomfortable. That's the very last thing I want to do."

Fucking James. Were you allowed to think that at someone's funeral? I wasn't sure, but it was beyond my ability to stop. All this time, and James had been in contact with Maddie. Had Kerry known this the whole time, too? Had everyone been meeting up with Maddie? Had they gone on holiday together, thrown parties without me?

"So you know I live in Box?" Had James revealed it all? Given her my street and house number?

She shook her head. "Not until just now. The place we're doing up — and where I'm staying occasionally — is in the Royal Crescent."

"Of course it is." That came out just as snarky as I intended. The most salubrious address in Bath, and Maddie had a flat there.

"It's not glamorous like you're thinking. When I'm there, I'm living among the dust. My blow-up mattress is far from living the high life. On the plus side, the commute is a synch. On the down side, the planning is taking forever, seeing as it's a listed building and we can't sneeze inside without asking the council."

I wasn't interested in small talk with Maddie. I downed the rest of my wine and stood up. "Well, this has been lovely, but I need a refill."

I spun around and rushed to the bar, getting another wine, trying to quell the shake of my limbs, the rush of my blood.

There was a murmur around the room and I turned to see Kerry and Gemma walking slowly across the carpet, carrying a cake almost as big as them. A bright purple rocket that held more than a hint of the phallic about it. Was this James's message from beyond the grave, telling us he was actually gay all along? That brought a smile to my face.

Nothing would surprise me today.

I walked over to my two friends. The cake now safely deposited, both stood back to admire it. Up close, I could see the intricate work that had gone into the small planets surrounding the rocket, as well as the flames shooting out the bottom, and the image of James waving from the cockpit.

That actually floored me, and I put a hand on Gemma's arm. I'd seen the cake in its early guises, but Gemma had taken it home to finish it off. "It's amazing, Gem. Did you cry making it?" Silly question, she was crying now.

Whereas my tear ducts were still unused, bone dry.

"What do you think?" she asked.

I squeezed her arm. "James would be very grateful and proud." I paused. "Either that, or he'd have cut into it already before we had a chance to take photos." I got my phone out immediately and did just that. Our Instagram feed deserved this one, and I got it before any damage was done.

"Thank you, Gem. James would love it." Kerry blew her nose into a tissue, before grabbing a glass of wine from the buffet table and raising it. "Everyone!" she shouted, snagging the room's attention in an instant. She put a hand on her diaphragm before she spoke. "Just to let you know, this cake was James's dying wish. A strange final request for a rocket cake, but that was James — unique to the last." She raised her eyes to the ceiling. "Wherever you are, honey, I hope you love it, just like I'll always love you."

My legs almost buckled when she said that, but instead I gripped my wine glass tight. I heard sniffles, and turned to see Maddie dabbing her eyes. Anger flared inside me.

I still hadn't cried, and it was all because of her.

Chapter Four

We walked back to Kerry's house after going for a Chinese meal in the village. My brogues dangled from one hand. They'd been a pain point all day, and I'd decided to take charge.

It was dark as we turned into her Bristol housing estate, but still warm enough for short sleeves. Neat rows of houses, white picket fences, paths up to freshly painted front doors, perfectly slanted roofs. I'd always laughed about such places when I was growing up, yet now I was developing a soft spot for them. Everything had its place in a setting like this, and when I'd arrived last night, I'd found it comforting. I always did when I visited Kerry and James.

Now just Kerry. That was going to take some getting used to.

Gemma had her arm through mine, and kept telling me how much she loved me and our business. We'd taken the leap and opened our cake school, Cake Heaven, five years ago. After a rocky first two years where we struggled to balance the books, we were now considering moving to a bigger space because demand for our classes was growing every month.

"I wish someone gorgeous would walk into one of our classes — a woman for you, and whoever for me. People think bisexuals have the pick of the land, but they couldn't be more wrong. I just want to meet someone I get on with. How fucking hard can it be?"

I kissed Gemma's cheek, laughing as I always did about society's view of bisexuals. That they were greedy and unfaithful. Gemma couldn't be further from that unfair stereotype. She was gorgeous and anybody would be lucky to have her, whatever their gender.

"But it's the law of averages, isn't it?" I turned to Gemma. "The first building block in your life is your home. The second is your relationship. The third is your career. And the law states that you can't be happy with all three at once, otherwise where's the drama?"

"That's a shit law."

"Agreed, but it's a universally acknowledged one. We're both doing well in our careers and home, but not so much in love." I paused, fishing out Kerry's key that she'd given me at the restaurant. We were the first to arrive back, the rest still not having made it as far as her road.

"Look at Kerry, she'll confirm it. Her and James were going along just fine. Picture-perfect house." I pushed open the red front door and walked into the lounge. "Matching decor, good jobs, and they loved each other. The universe ignored them for a while, letting them have their fun. Then, bam!" I snapped my fingers. "The universe did a stock take, had a conference and gave James cancer." I flicked the lights on. The kitchen was just as we'd left it the night before when we'd stayed over to support Kerry, the wine we'd brought with us lined up on the counter. "Now, she's got a house that's paid off, a job she enjoys, but no husband. You can't have it all."

"You're a doom-monger tonight, you know that?"

"Just calling it how I see it." I got the corkscrew out and opened a bottle of Shiraz, before grabbing a bottle of Pinot Grigio from Kerry's fridge. Her cat Hercules stirred from his favourite place by the kitchen window, and walked around my legs, meowing as he did. I bent to pet him, but as soon as I did, he ran away. Cats.

"So you're seriously telling me I can't have all three?" Gemma frowned, fiddling with her hair again. She had so much hair spray on it, I swear it hadn't moved all day. "That's bullshit. I know plenty of people who do."

"Maybe you only think they do. They probably don't."

"Your mum and dad for a start. They love each other."

"But neither of them likes their jobs."

"Your mum does."

My mum worked at Marks & Spencer's. She loved her workmates, but she hated her management, describing them all as "a bunch of eejits." She tended to slip into her natural Irish brogue when it came to them. Dad had told her to stop working if she wanted, but she liked being needed. Now both her children had left home, that only happened at her job. So she stayed.

The real reason she kept it was because she enjoyed having someone to chat at all day — customers or workmates, she wasn't fussy. Also, she loved the discounted food the staff got. Every time I went home, she proudly showed off her latest bargain to me. "Will you look, Justine," she'd say. "Two chicken breasts in a mustard and cream sauce for 99p. And it was £3.75. Now that's a saving!" Mum lived for those moments.

"She likes bits of it; my dad hates his. But he'll never leave, because he understands the universal law. He'd rather have a wife and a roof over his head than have a satisfying job." My dad was a plumber, and as he always told me, nobody wanted to stick their hands down toilets for a living if they were honest. He did it because he liked the freedom it gave him. Plus, he liked that people paid him handsomely for sticking his hands down their toilets.

Gemma fixed me with her disbelieving stare as she thought about it. "That doesn't fill me with hope for the rest of my life, seeing as I love my job and my flat."

"Maybe we should try to flout it this year. We both love our jobs, we both like where we live. So let's see if we can outsmart this law."

"You think we could?" Gemma's face told me she was in doubt.

"It'll only come true if you really believe."

"Like Santa?"

I laughed. I knew Gemma still watched Christmas movies in May. "Yes, just like Santa." I paused. "The thing is, I'd quite like a girlfriend and so would you. If either of us died tomorrow, friends and family would turn up, but we wouldn't have a significant other. Someone to sit in the front bench and sob their heart out. Someone to prove we were truly loved."

Gemma thought for a moment. "Maddie would turn up and be sad at yours."

I slapped her arm. "Great, an ex from 10 years ago. I'm surprised my insides haven't shrivelled up and died."

"Maisy would come."

"And bring her new wife and baby?" Maisy was my most recent ex, and we'd split up three years ago. "It's fucking depressing. If I died, nobody's life would be severely impacted. Nobody's daily routine would change."

Gemma prodded her chest with her index finger. "Er, hello? We work together on a daily basis. I think my routine might be a little altered."

"You know what I mean. I don't have a lover, a chief mourner. Someone to sit in the front row of the crematorium who's not my parents or my annoying brother."

"If you die, I promise to be in the front row crying buckets. Can you say the same, Mrs No Tears?" Gemma furrowed her brow to show how likely she thought that would be.

I put myself in the front row and screwed up my face. Gemma was dead, and I was at her funeral. "I'd totally cry for you."

"You're such a bad liar."

She knew me too well. "But we need to sort the universe out. We need to make it love us and break the law."

"I'm normally law-abiding, but I'm happy to break this one." Gemma paused. "Just to be clear. We're going to be more on the lookout for love so that when we die, we'll have a chief mourner?"

"I've heard of worse reasons."

A banging on the front door interrupted our conversation.

"Thank god for that. This conversation was getting weird." Gemma left the room and came back moments later with the rest of the group, including James's school friends, whose names I still hadn't learned. One of them looked like a Dave, but I wasn't going to christen him unduly. But there was normally a Dave. That was another law.

The energy rushed as people poured into the kitchen, the air filling with chatter and the creak of cupboard doors.

"Did you get any pink wine, Kerry?" A lady in pink asked that. Julie? Jenny? Janet? She was wearing a pink dress, with pink earrings and pink shoes. And she drank pink wine. I bet if she got her phone out, the cover would be pink. Her vibrator probably was, too.

Kerry fished the rosé from her wine fridge and pink lady gave her a grin the width of the M25.

A hiss of a lager can opening near me signalled Rob had found his stash of Stella. Maddie stood awkwardly in the kitchen doorway, Hercules mewling around her feet.

"Drink?" Rob asked, holding up his can.

Maddie nodded. "That'd be great." Her eyes caught mine briefly, then she looked away.

What was it about being around her? She drew me in and repelled me all at the same time, like some kind of magnet gone wrong. It was more than a little confusing. I wanted to run, yet I wanted to stare.

I picked up my glass of Pinot Grigio, moving to the back door. I stepped out into the garden, lit by the glare of the kitchen light. It looked a little overgrown, a sign of how ill James had been. When he was alive, he'd been a keen gardener.

I took a huge gulp of air and tipped my head up to the inky sky above. I could make out a couple of stars, but that was it. Even in the Somerset countryside, light pollution put paid to that.

The back door creaked open and I looked up to see Maddie, cigarette in hand. She grimaced as she stepped onto the patio. "Do you mind?" She gestured with the fag in her hand. Without waiting for my answer, she put down her can of Stella, and placed the cigarette between her lips.

"Yes, I fucking do," I wanted to say, but didn't.

Instead, being English, I smiled and nodded. It appeared whether I minded or not, she was out here with me, lighting her fag.

* * *

"Can you see Orion's Belt?" Maddie stood beside me, a heady mix of musky perfume and her. She still smelled the same, and it took me right back to when we were dating. The same thing happened whenever Justin Timberlake's 'SexyBack' came on the radio. It had been our song. Whenever I heard it, no matter where I was or who I was with, I always thought of Maddie. The song took me back to happier times when all we wanted was to take on the world, side by side. Was it the same for her, or had she squelched every part of us from her memory bank when she'd walked away?

"Too cloudy." I kept my gaze pointed upwards. Out of the corner of my eye, Maddie's cigarette burnt orange in the darkness as she took a drag.

"Remember we used to stargaze at uni?"

Did she really think I'd forgotten? "Of course. You showed them to me. You were a secret stargazer, eager to share your knowledge."

She laughed. "I was a bit of a nerd, wasn't I?"

"A sweet nerd." For a moment, I forgot I was mad at her. Maddie Kind. Only, she hadn't been all that kind in the end.

A few seconds went by as we stared upwards.

Then Maddie spoke. "Shit thing to happen to James."

Stupid thing to say. "Yep."

"You think he's looking down on us?"

"Are you saying you think James is in heaven?"

Maddie chuckled. "I don't know about heaven, but

maybe he's... somewhere?" She paused, reaching into her pocket. She pulled out her packet of fags and offered it to me.

I stared, then took one. I'd given up smoking seven years ago. Yet something about tonight, something about this moment felt right to smoke. We'd smoked like chimneys when we were students. If I had to add up the amount of time Maddie and I spent smoking, chatting, holding hands and looking up at the stars... well, it would run into days, maybe weeks.

"If you are looking down," Maddie said, inhaling like a pro. "Here's to you, James." She raised her cigarette. "And by the way, it was a fuckwit move to go and die."

I smiled at that.

Maddie fixed me with her stare. Even in the moonlight, the whites of her eyes bored into me. "But we've all pulled fuckwit moves in our lives, haven't we?"

I let her statement linger in the air like a waft of stale perfume. "Some more than others."

She looked down briefly, and took another drag on her cigarette. She stared straight ahead.

"I can't believe you still smoke. Even with all those warnings on the pack. I gave up seven years ago."

She shook her head. "I don't as a rule. Only when I'm nervous."

"I make you nervous?"

"Apparently, you do." She paused. "I know it's a bit late in the day, but I'm sorry about everything, Jus."

I coughed. Maddie was apologising. At one stage in my life, I had wanted nothing more than for Maddie to turn up at my door and beg for my forgiveness. I'd wanted it for a good year, and my response would have changed every few months.

From months one to three, I would have screamed at her, cried, and then probably ended up in bed.

From months four to six, I would have punched her in the face, screamed and then probably ended up in bed.

From months seven to nine, I would have cried, wailed, got angry and ended up in bed.

However, by month ten, and certainly by the time the year was up, I would have told her to do one and slammed the door in her face.

But now, we were on year 10. That was 122 months since she'd vanished, like the best type of magician ever. My response after so many years? I was sad, but nothing more. No wailing, punching or crying. Because it didn't matter. We were different people with different lives now. Even so, still being in the same proximity of Maddie left me exposed.

"You should be." I turned to face her. "Are you going to fill me in? On why you vanished without a trace?"

She turned her face skywards again, blowing out smoke in a straight line. "Cold feet. Fear of commitment." She paused. "I saw our future flash before my eyes and it scared the shit out of me."

"So you just upped and left? Didn't I deserve a little

more than that, having been your girlfriend for nearly four years?"

She nodded. "You deserved it all. And I, stupid shit that I was, deserved nothing. That's what I got. I think that's what I believed, so I thought I'd commit it to a self-fulfilling prophecy before it actually happened." She paused. "If it makes any difference, I've regretted it every day since."

A ball of anger hurtled up my system. All this time I'd wondered why, worried about what I'd done, and it turned out to be just a classic fear of commitment? Just Maddie and her belief that things wouldn't work out? If I hadn't wanted to slap her before, now I truly did. I refrained, though. We were still at a wake. I kept my hands by my side, even though my left fist was clenched so hard, my nails were going to leave marks on my skin. I took a deep breath before I responded.

"And how's life worked out for you since then? Have you committed with someone else?"

She shook her head, throwing her cigarette butt on the floor and grinding it under foot. "Nope. I don't think my attitude changed for quite some time. When that's the case, you give off vibes. Women came and went. And now, well, other things have become more important."

I held up my hand. "I don't need to know details."

"There's been nobody since you. Not in the same way." She paused. "How about you? I don't see a ring."

"I'm sure James kept you up to date with my love life."

I was getting snarky again. But then, I wasn't going to tell her the truth. That she'd ruined me with her lies, and now trust wasn't high on the list of things I was good at. I'd mastered many things in the intervening years: beef wellington, tarte tatin, painting a ceiling without falling off a ladder. But, since Maddie, trusting someone with my heart had proved beyond me.

She shook her head. "Not really. James was protective of you, of how I'd treated you, and I understood that. So we stuck to safer topics, and let that one lie."

"It still seems surreal he's gone."

"I know," she replied. "He was my link to you lot, and I treasured it and him. He used to try to persuade me to come along to the uni get-togethers," Maddie added. "He told me you'd be fine with it, seeing as it was quite a few years on."

"So why didn't you?" I wouldn't have been fine with it.

Maddie shrugged, taking another slug of her beer. "I never thought I had the right. I thought I'd have to get your written permission, and talking to you after all that time seemed like a big ask. So I never came."

"But here we are," I replied. "James had an extreme way of getting us to talk, in the end."

"He did."

Maddie cleared her throat before she spoke, turning her gaze fully on me. "I hope this isn't a one-off, though. I'd like to come along for drinks next time, but only if you're cool with it."

The question dangled like a spider web between us, glinting in the moonlight. If I walked anywhere near it, I'd be caught in her web. Maddie's web.

Because of that, my feet stayed rooted to the spot.

Yes, it might be 122 months since she walked out the door, but it didn't mean I wanted her to walk right back. There was a protocol here, and thankfully, Maddie was acknowledging it.

Would I ever be cool with it? I looked down at the cigarette, still unlit in my hand. I wasn't the same person she'd left a decade ago, and that showed it.

Would I be cool with Maddie walking back into my world? My initial reaction was: not in this lifetime.

Chapter Five

The phones at Cake Heaven were going batshit crazy this morning. This normally happened after an episode of the 'Great British Bake Off'. I was pretty sure our business would have thrived without that show working its magic, but with it on our side, we couldn't fail.

Last night's episode had focused on sugar-free cakes, which we weren't about to offer a class in. That was a fad that would pass, we hoped. People wanted to still eat cake, but they didn't seem to realise the alternatives also contained calories. Sugar wasn't the demon it was branded, and it was one of the five pillars of Cake Heaven. The others being eggs, butter, flour and nuclear-strength coffee. I'd been slugging back coffee all morning while I decorated my dummy cakes that were going to be used in our new window displays.

"Why are the phones ringing off the hook when I really need to get these cakes done this morning?" The question was to Gemma, who'd just come in from the wholesalers, and was currently hauling industrial-sized bags of sugar and flour on a metal trolley.

"That's not a bad thing." Gemma dropped a bag of flour onto the aluminium shelves that lined the back wall of the kitchen.

Our space in Bristol had been perfect when we'd started, and I still loved the kitchen, mainly due to the giant roof lantern which flooded the room with sunlight. In fact, even when it was chucking it down, I still loved baking with the rain falling on the panes overhead, the drama of the weather fuelling my work. The first kitchen I'd ever seen with a skylight was in Maddie's mum's house, and I knew then I wanted that in my future. I chewed my cheek at the thought of Maddie. Not this morning.

The only downside to our current location was we were quickly outgrowing it, and so we were in a dilemma: should we move the whole show to a new premises, or should we open up a second site and split ourselves in two? It was a question Gemma and I had been pondering for a while, but we still hadn't found anywhere perfect for either scenario.

For now, we were plodding along as if nothing was wrong. Gemma was all for branching out, but money was a sticking point. I was naturally more cautious than her; as too, it seemed, were the banks. We were pretty sure it was because we were women in our thirties and they thought we were going to have kids and bugger off any minute. I'd never realised how sexist the world was until I started my own business and it hit me full in the face.

"How's it going?" Gemma put her bag on the stainless-steel work surface and let out a sigh, before walking to the coffee machine and pouring herself a coffee from the pot I'd made half an hour ago. "You want one?"

I shook my head. "I just had one and I need to keep on, I'm in flow." Our photographer, Chrissy — super-talented and super-gorgeous — was coming in to photograph the new tiered cakes I was showcasing for a class we were about to offer, called Super-Hot Cakes. The class was set to feature all the latest decorating techniques, including perfect drip, along with edible feathers and sails. We also showed students how to make salted caramel buttercream, along with the boss of icing: Swiss meringue buttercream. Gemma or I took all the shots we needed for social media, but when it came to the website, we relied on Chrissy, who worked for cash and a side of cake.

This dummy cake was for show purposes only and after being photographed would sit in our window. I had an edible cake ready to feed Chrissy when she got here, too. That one was vanilla sponge, Swiss meringue buttercream interior and chocolate ganache on the outside, topped with home-made chocolate truffles. My stomach rumbled just looking at it.

Gemma gave me a smile. "You're bloody good at those, you know. Those sails look incredible. Shame I can't have any with my coffee." The 'sails' were pink Candy Melts spread and set over bubble wrap to create a waffle effect; and vanilla Candy Melts set into wide shards with multi-coloured sprinkles.

"It wouldn't taste very good." I returned her grin. "This

one's nearly done, two more after this." I glanced up at the clock. 11:15 am. Two more hours until Chrissie turned up after lunch. It should be plenty of time.

"One other thing." Gemma put down her coffee. "I take it you haven't checked your phone this morning?" Her tone made me look up. When I saw her face, I stilled.

"No. Why?"

"You know Maddie was still at Kerry's when we left, the morning after the funeral?"

I nodded. We'd left soon after we woke up, as we had a property to view. Plus, the last thing I'd wanted was to have breakfast with Maddie. "I do."

"She helped Kerry out with a particular task." She paused. "Of driving her to the chemist to get a pregnancy kit. Apparently, Kerry had just assumed her period was late because of all the stress of James dying."

"Understandably." The blood drained from my face as my mind connected the dots.

Gemma sucked on the inside of her cheek. "The upshot is, she's very much pregnant. With her dead husband's baby."

"Oh my god." I dropped the piping bag I was holding, washed my hands and went to retrieve my phone. When I picked it up, I smeared icing on the screen. Like I did every single time.

Sure enough, there it was in our WhatsApp group. A message from Kerry telling us she was just over three months pregnant. Of all the people to break the news to, it'd been Maddie. The day after her husband's funeral. "Fuck me, poor Kerry. First James, now this. Why is she only just telling us?" It'd been three days since James's funeral, and those days must have seemed like years to Kerry after this news.

Gemma gave a small shrug. "I called her. She said she just needed time for it to sink in. Plus, she's been staying with her parents since she found out, so she's had support. Her mum's taking her away to a spa hotel this weekend — that was planned all along. But when she gets back, she's going to need our support more than ever."

"Three months, though. Did she not think she might be?"

"She said she was putting off testing, she didn't want to know. She and James managed a final hurrah together, but she was convinced the treatment would have buggered up his sperm."

"Shouldn't she be showing by now? I didn't think she looked pregnant."

Gemma shrugged. "I'm no expert on being pregnant, but I guess it varies. And possibly your husband dying during the baby's initial growth might put some stress on how that goes. Who knows." She licked her lips. "I was thinking I might drive over there next weekend, just to give her a hug and cook her dinner or whatever she needs. Do you want to come, too?"

I nodded. "Count me in." I took a deep breath. "Months ago, who would have thought this could happen? That

James would be dead and Kerry would be having his baby?"

"Just goes to show you've got to live your best life while you can, every day." Gemma nodded her head towards me. "Which you're doing with that icing."

Chapter Six

Going back to Kerry's two weeks after the funeral was still odd. You couldn't come here and not see and feel James. Would that fade over time? I hoped not. As Gemma pulled her car into Kerry's driveway, she swore under her breath. Because there, in front of us, was a red Mini both of us recognised. Still shiny. Still boy-racer. It was the funeral all over again.

"Kerry knew we were coming, right? You told her it was today?" Instantly, I went from feeling hungry to like I never wanted to eat again. Maddie had asked if I'd be okay with her coming back into our group. Here was my answer.

Gemma stopped the car and turned her head. "Yes. But Maddie was there when she found out, so I guess she came over to see if Kerry was okay. She's just being nice, and I guess there's no timetable for that, is there?"

My heart did a backflip, then a forward roll as I contemplated my options. I could demand that Gemma reverse out of the driveway, careful not to run over the myriad of children currently playing football on the estate.

I could let out a loud scream — we were in the car, and, being in business together, Gemma and I had witnessed each other freaking out many times. Or, I could handle this like the grown-up I really didn't think I was and deal with Maddie. Because it seemed Maddie was going to be back in my life whether I liked it or not.

Just as I was deciding to be grown-up and adult, Kerry's front door opened. She and Maddie appeared. Kerry was laughing at something Maddie said, and then she gave her a big hug. Not just a small one, but a hug that said Maddie had done something lovely for her and she appreciated it.

Perhaps it was because Maddie had taken time out of her day to come and see her. That wasn't the action of a callous woman who walked out on her girlfriend without a word. Although maybe there were different rules for lovers and friends in Maddie's world. Or perhaps I had no idea who she was or what she valued anymore, seeing as I'd only spent a handful of minutes with her in the past decade.

Gemma starting the car interrupted my thoughts. Before I knew it, we reversed slowly out of the drive and parked up on the kerb. When she cut the engine, I gave Gemma a look.

She shook her head. "You're getting out, you can't hide in here. You know that, right?"

I sighed, doing as I was told. The sound of our car doors slamming shut were like gun shots in my head.

Maddie was hovering by her Mini. She raised her hand in greeting.

Gemma walked over to her, car keys in one hand, dragging me along with her spare hand.

"Good to see you again." Maddie gave Gemma a kiss on the cheek, but hung back on doing the same to me, settling instead on an unsure smile. She couldn't get close anyway, seeing as I was carrying the chocolate ganache cake I'd made earlier — Kerry's favourite.

"You, too," Gemma replied. "You just leaving?"

Maddie nodded. "I have to get back — family calls. But I wanted to check Kerry was okay. I know how it is after someone close to you dies and the funeral's over. Everyone else goes back to normal, apart from you. Grief makes your world constrict. I just want to make sure Kerry's doesn't do that." Her gaze landed on my face, and she left it there for a few seconds, then looked away, shaking herself. "Anyway, she seems good, and I'm sure having you both here will cheer her right up." She moved towards her car. "Have a good evening."

She gave us a smile I couldn't decipher, gave Kerry another wave and then she was gone.

Kerry gave us both hugs as we walked in, before glancing at me. "Before you say anything, I didn't know she was coming today."

I raised an eyebrow. "You haven't been having secret meetings for months like James?"

"No, I haven't." She kissed my cheek, before pushing her fair curls behind her ears. They sprang out again immediately. Kerry had the unruliest hair I'd ever seen, and I wondered if her baby would inherit the same. "But you brought cake, so let's talk about that instead." She paused. "And dinner is on James tonight. I even ordered a really lovely bottle of champagne you can have. Not me, obviously." She patted her not-very-obviously pregnant belly, concealed under a floaty orange and yellow sundress. "But I wanted someone to enjoy some bubbles after the news I had yesterday. But a cup of tea first?"

We walked through to the kitchen and Gemma put the kettle on, watching Kerry the whole time. "So what news have you had?"

I put the cake on the worktop and turned to face our host.

Kerry clutched the worktop behind her. "That I'm bloody rich. I mean, by my standards, bonkers rich. Turns out that James had all these policies set up and they're paying out. He wasn't ill when he took them out, and they were all payable on death. You never think you're going to need them, and most people don't. But for me, this is huge. Bittersweet, but still." She hung her head for a moment, before rallying, giving us a smile.

We took our teas through to the lounge and sat while we processed what Kerry had said. Her biscuit-coloured carpet was springy under foot. She and James had only picked out the teal-blue matching sofas the year before. Beside the large TV was a framed photo of their wedding day, the smiles on their faces so perfect, so unaware of what was ahead. But as Kerry had said on the night before the funeral, she'd still had 13 great years with James, six of them as his wife. She'd never be sorry about that.

"How much are you talking?" Gemma never was one to beat around the bush.

"The mortgage is paid off, and I never have to work again if I don't want to. I mean, I probably will carry on for the moment, but it means I don't have to worry so much when the baby's born. James had thought of everything, bless his macabre ways." She paused. "And if you'll let me, I want to spend some money on you both, too."

"Fantastic. What were you thinking? A yacht each?" Gemma laughed at her own joke, waiting for Kerry to do the same.

When she didn't, I reached over and touched her arm. "We don't want your money. We're your friends, and you should keep it for you and your baby's future."

Kerry smiled, and I could see the emotion in her eyes. This had to be hard. She was rich, but she'd lost the one who mattered most. "Oh, I know that, and I'm not being frivolous with it. I want to invest it. In stocks, in products and in businesses." She took a deep breath and looked at me, then at Gemma. "And the first business I want to make a difference in is yours."

Hang on a minute, what had she just said? My heart swelled with anticipation, and I strained my ears to hear what Kerry was going to say next.

Gemma put a hand to her chest. "Ours?"

Kerry nodded. "Yes. I've sat and listened to you talking

about how sexist banks are, and how you need money to expand. Well I've got that money now, so let me be your bank. I'm not giving you it. It's an investment. But mainly, I just want to help my best friends out. It's an interest-free loan. You've both been brilliant throughout this whole nightmare of a year. Now let's make something good come from James's death, and use the money he left to help you two take Cake Heaven to the next level. And then perhaps the one after that. What do you say?"

I glanced at Gemma and was pleased to see she was wearing the exact same stunned expression I was. For the second time in the past half hour, I wanted to scream, but this time for a positive reason. Yes, I was still scared of moving forward with the business. However, with this barrier down, I was going to have to face my fears.

Gemma was the first to react. "What do we say? We say that's fucking amazing. Right, Jus?"

I nodded. "It's so generous. Are you sure?"

Kerry nodded. "Never been surer of anything. I want to live well and to do that, I have to honour James and what he would have wanted. He'd be thrilled his money was going to Cake Heaven; both to help you, and to bring more cake into the world." Kerry took hold of one of my hands, and one of Gemma's. "He loved you two. He loved us all. It's perfect, don't you think?"

I loved James, too, and I still missed him every day. In a second, we were all stood in a huddle, arms entwined. "I love you both," I said, squeezing tight.

There are those moments in life that are naturally sweet, and this was one of them. I felt it in my bones and in my heart; I felt it pulsing in my blood. Then an image of Maddie popped into my head, her eyes so sad when she spoke about loss. Who had she lost? Someone special? Someone for whom she was still grieving? No matter how crazed she made me feel, I wouldn't wish that on anyone.

When we released each other and pulled back, smiles wide, there were tears glistening on Gemma and Kerry's cheeks. Of course there were. But my own were dry, just as they'd been for a decade. I didn't need to touch them to be sure. Gemma and Kerry got a tissue to blow their noses.

Meanwhile, I blew out a long breath. "You're really going to lend us money?" Our business was growing every day thanks to the wonder of Instagram and Gemma's video skills, and we needed to find a way to monetise and stop turning business away. If Kerry lent us cash, perhaps our moving dream could become a reality.

She nodded. "I really am. I want to help with the down payment on your business. I want you both to fly. Then once that's sorted, we can turn our attention to your love lives."

I shook my head and looked at Gemma. "I'm not sure that's such an easy fix. You can't just go to an auction and get yourself a woman like you can a property, can you? Plus, I'm not sure I'd want to seeing as all sales are final. It's a bit of a commitment."

Kerry laughed. "I promise I won't sell you to the nearest cartel, okay? But seriously, lending you money for the business will give me a focus, too. I'll take extra interest in how you're getting on." She paused, her face a question mark. "So, you're on board?"

"Of course we're on board!" Gemma replied.

I laughed. "How could we not be? Thank you, Kerry. You're amazing." To be thinking of others at a time when she must be wanting to crawl under her duvet and hide? It showed what a fantastic person she was. "We won't let you down, will we?"

Gemma was already shaking her head. "No way. This is added impetus to make it work, not that we wouldn't anyway. Cake Heaven is going to be the name on everyone's lips by the time we're done."

"And I know it'll taste delicious, just like all your cake, so it's a no-brainer." Kerry sat back, groaning as she did.

"How are you feeling, anyway?" I asked.

Suddenly, she looked tired. "Fine. The pregnancy is wiping me out a bit, but that's normal. James's mum keeps coming around to check on me. The other night, I hid under the window ledge and pretended I wasn't in, even though my car was there. I know people are trying to be kind and make sure I'm okay, but sometimes I just need some time on my own. Netflix, cup of tea, Wispa."

She smiled. "I answered the door earlier thinking it was you two, but it was Maddie. It was sweet of her to call round." Kerry glanced at me. "I know things are weird between you two, but she's been so supportive and understanding. That's the kind of person I need in my life at the moment."

I swallowed down the reply on the tip of my tongue and kept my game face on. If Kerry was finding Maddie a good ally, then I was pleased. She needed everyone she could in her corner. So long as Maddie steered clear of my corner, I was fine with it. Kind of. I turned to our silent partner. "Did you say the champagne was on ice? Would now be a good time to open it?"

She gave me a grin. "Now would be the ideal time to open it." Kerry got up and strode to the kitchen, the fridge opening with a squeak just like always.

I turned to Gemma. "I can't believe this is happening. We're getting money and we can start to expand."

Gemma nodded, blinking rapidly. "I know."

Kerry appeared at the kitchen doorway, champagne in hand. "Are you any good at opening these?"

I jumped up. "Champagne-opener is my middle name." Within seconds the bottle was popped and the glasses filled, and the three of us were on our feet. It had only been two weeks since the funeral, but today was a day of hope in Kerry's lounge. So different to what had been.

"I'm just going to have a sip," Kerry said. "I don't want baby getting drunk so early on." She smiled down at her stomach. "To an expanding me, and an expanding Cake Heaven. James would have loved both of them." Her jaw wobbled as she spoke.

I took her hand and raised my glass. "To James, to Cake Heaven, but mostly, to you."

Gemma leaned in and kissed Kerry's cheek. "Thanks for your faith, and thank for your investment. We promise not to fuck it up."

Chapter Seven

Cupcake Masterclass was a hugely popular weekend class, and today we were bracing ourselves for a 14-strong hen party. Gemma and I had spent last night getting everything prepared so that I could have a bit of a Saturday lie-in. These days, that was anything past 7:00 am. How my university self would have scoffed.

I pulled my green Golf — named Kermit — into the parking space at the back of our studio, slammed the car door and stretched my back. The sun was strong in the sky even at 9:00 am. I pushed my Ray Bans up my nose and grabbed my black leather bag from the back seat. My Golf was a car I'd always wanted in my teens, and now I was in my thirties and could afford it, it was one of my first things I'd acquired. I still couldn't quite afford a house, but I was renting one from a friend who gave me mate's rates. Plus, I was saving for a deposit so I could buy my own as soon as I could, perhaps in Bristol where prices were cheaper.

I was the first one in, with Gemma taking today off. We took it in turns to take the weekend classes, and today Amisha was my helper, who was an uber-keen baker.

I smiled as I assessed our space. Dazzling sunshine bathed the studio from the floor-to-ceiling windows, and the long wooden-topped workbenches looked fresh and inviting, waiting to get messed up with flour, butter, and colour gels. The benches were topped with branded Cake Heaven aprons, along with mixers lined up in rows, a line of pastel colours ready for action.

When I'd first started teaching baking classes, I'd been winging it. But now, having been doing it for the past few years, I was confident I'd be able to deal with whatever the class threw at me. Most of our clients had some level of competency, but some were complete novices. My favourite part of the job was giving people the extra skills and confidence to take their baking to the next level. That confidence would then invariably have a knock-on effect on the rest of their lives, too.

I hoped at least some of today's class were up for baking as well as a good time, but you never could tell with hen parties. They were always such a fuse of dynamics, with workmates, family and friends thrown together, often for the first time. Mix in the stress of weddings and the fact that all they really wanted to do was drink, and hen parties were sometimes more trouble than they were worth.

I thought back to one particular party last month. Within the first hour, the bride had been in tears over something the group had done. We'd spent the next hour berating men and making tea, trying to calm the bride down. When I'd eventually got them all baking, they'd paid attention for a while. That is, until the prosecco had been demanded early, and then all bets were off. I'd ended up decorating half the cakes so the party had something they could take home. I was crossing my fingers today's group wouldn't be such a headache.

It'd been six weeks since the funeral, and after the shock of seeing Maddie, I was back on an even keel. The bottom hadn't fallen out of my world. Yes, I'd been shaken initially, but now I felt I could cope. I'd got over the driveway incident, and hearing Kerry talk about Maddie made me realise maybe she wasn't such a bad person anymore.

Plus, it turned out, I was better at this shit than I'd given myself credit for. The intervening years had upped my resilience, and Gemma had been right. I was a badass. Perhaps I should get it emblazoned on an apron for my future classes, just in case anyone was in any doubt.

I flicked on the lights in the kitchen and put some coffee on — the most important part of any day. I'd just filled the machine with water when Amisha strolled in, giving me a broad smile. She was carrying a tray of vagina cupcakes, which tasted better than they looked. Vagina cupcakes meant today's hen party was lesbian. I'd forgotten that. I wasn't a fan of the current trend for genital-themed cupcakes, but whenever there was a hen party, this was us catering to the crowd. I didn't want to spend my day piping buttercream onto a sponge vulva, but as long as we supplied them ready-made, it scratched the itch. The hens then had time to make cupcakes with artistry they could show to their mother.

My heart fluttered as it always did when I realised it was a lesbian crowd. We were getting lesbian hen parties more often these days, which was brilliant. However, I was always worried they would involve someone I knew. Or, more to the point, someone I'd slept with over the past decade. Not that I was a slut of the highest order, but I had slept with a handful of women. Maybe two handfuls.

"You've made the cupcakes. Have I told you lately that I love you?"

"I even made one for both of us, so sixteen vagina cupcakes in all." Amisha had dyed her hair again. This time, she'd gone metallic green.

I laughed. "I'm sure they're going to be a big hit."

Amisha was like an angel sent from baking heaven. She'd arrived at our door two years ago as a client for one of our advanced decorating classes, and had never truly left. After that first class, she stayed behind and we'd chatted over a coffee. She loved baking and asked if we needed any help. At that point, we didn't. She'd kept in touch popping in every so often to let us know she was still available, and six months down the line I'd asked her to help with a weekend class. Now she was a freelance member of staff. She'd taken her first solo class about six months ago and had been a big hit, but she was equally happy to be my number two when needed. Like today.

Amisha was only five foot, but what she lacked in height, she more than made up for in enthusiasm. It was infectious, and she could eulogise about cake for hours. She'd applied to the 'Great British Bake Off' three times with no success. If she did ever get on, I was sure the great British public would fall in love with her instantly. Plus, for the amount of cake she made and ate, she was surprisingly slim. I assumed it was her nervous energy. Amisha never sat still.

"I can't wait to see their faces. I love it when they realise what the cupcakes are. Plus, you know me, I love a good hen party." Amisha put the cupcakes on the side, before grabbing two mugs from the cupboard as the coffee began to drip through.

"This is a mega hen party. Fourteen guests. That's a whole lot of organisation for some poor sap." I folded my arms across my chest. "They wanted to bring 20 hens, but I told them we couldn't accommodate that." I sucked on my top lip. "Which only makes it even more brilliant that Kerry is investing in the business. Soon we won't have to turn down the bigger groups. All that's needed is to find that elusive location for a better and bigger Cake Heaven."

Gemma was already on the case, registering interest with agents and scouring auction brochures. She had left some options on the side yesterday, but I hadn't had a chance to study them yet, to see if the locations worked. Ensuring our clients could find Cake Heaven easily was key, so it had to be within striking distance of good transport links and have ample parking. We didn't want to spend half our day directing people and waiting for them to turn up. Even with the advent of smartphones and GPS, it still amazed me how many people couldn't follow a basic map.

The edges of Amisha's mouth turned downwards. "But I love it here. It's such a quaint location."

"I agree. We might yet keep this and get another location, who knows? But if we had bigger premises, we could have more and bigger classes."

Cake Heaven sat at the end of a residential street, on a site that had been converted from old garages. It was surrounded by a handful of shops, including The Bristol Bakery, run by one of my best friends, Rob — he of the husband and twins fame. The space was homely and in a hip Bristol neighbourhood, but there was no chance of expanding. Hence our dilemma.

"How come the hen party decided to come anyhow if we couldn't fit them all in?"

I pushed myself off the workbench and took the mug of coffee Amisha handed me. "Not sure. I'm guessing some of them decided they could live without knowing how to bake cupcakes? Whatever, we've still got a whole load of eager bakers turning up today. I just hope there's not too much drama and they haven't all slept with each other."

Amisha sucked in a breath. "You can't say that. Have you slept with all your queer friends?"

"Only half of them." I gave her a wink. "Joking." I paused. "Plus, I'm allowed to say that; I'm a lesbian."

"Whatever you say, boss." She was smiling as she spoke. "I'm sure it's going to be a great day."

I rubbed my hands together. "I am, too. Plus, a lesbian hen do means I'll have to crack out my lesbian jokes 101.

Did you put the fizz in the fridge?" For our hen parties, we treated the guests to cake and fizz at the end of the day. We also recommended a local restaurant for their meal afterwards, giving them money-off vouchers. It was a win-win for the local economy and for them.

Amisha nodded. "I did, so we're all set. Let me just grab the pastries from Rob for our welcome coffee, and then I'll start setting up the cups."

"Perfect."

Chapter Eight

If we were in any doubt about who the bride was, it was crystal clear when she walked through our doors half an hour later wearing a sparkly tiara. Her name was Brianna, and the hens were insistent on chanting her name at every opportunity, despite the fact it was only 9:45 am.

"Brianna! Brianna! Brianna!"

On the up side, Brianna appeared relaxed and not about to burst into tears about her future wife, which I was grateful for. More importantly, I didn't know a single person, mainly due to the fact they were from London. I gave up a silent prayer of thanks to the lesbian goddesses, who were clearly smiling down on me.

After taking everyone's coats and getting them sat behind their benches, we loaded the ladies up with coffee and pastries, which made them inordinately pleased. It was like nobody had ever given them coffee and pastries before. I was chatting to the chief bridesmaid, Helen — I guessed this was her role because she was wearing a T-shirt that said Chief Bridesmaid. Helen had an undercut and a fringe that fell into her eyes. She also had a nose ring, which I applauded. I'd tried one in my twenties, but quickly taken it out when I realised I couldn't blow my nose without snot escaping through it. Helen clearly had the nose ring thing mastered.

"Helen, sorry to interrupt." Amisha came up to us, and she really did look sorry. She was the sweetest person alive. "I was just wondering if we have more people coming? Only you booked for 14, but we've only got 10?"

Helen had a mouthful of pain au raisin and nodded, waving her phone in her right hand. "There's another car coming, but they had issues. They're going to be here but might be cutting it fine. They said to go ahead without them. Let me text them again." She set about doing just that.

I crooked my mouth. I didn't need the class interrupted, but then again, I didn't want to make an issue of it. This group were spending a good chunk of money with us today, and I wanted to make their experience perfect so they'd tell all their friends. Along with Instagram, word of mouth was our biggest source of business. "If you could find out, that'd be great. I'd rather wait until we're all here to start, so if we have to pour another cup of coffee, that's no problem."

But Helen's face broke into a smile. "They've just pulled into the city centre, so they should be here very soon. Their sat nav drove them the wrong way." She looked down into her empty mug. "But I wouldn't say no to another coffee."

Amisha grabbed the mug off her. "Coming right up."

"Can you tell them to park in the car park at the end of the road and not on the street. Cars get towed all the time here." Gemma had been towed three times, much to her chagrin.

Helen nodded, then sent a text. "Done," she replied.

The women were all in their 30s, apart from someone I assumed was the bride's mother or aunt. It was her who was currently waving her arms around in an excited manner and proclaiming that being here was "just like Bake Off!" We got that a lot.

"Right ladies!" I clapped my hands to get the group's attention. Even with only ten hens in the room, the volume was already ratcheted right up. It was only going to get louder as the day went on. "This is your final call to go to the loo and if anyone needs any more drinks, put your hand up and Amisha and I will assist you. Once the last few stragglers arrive, it'll be time to get baking!"

* * *

True to Helen's ETA, the doors to the studio sprang open around ten minutes later, and four women all kitted out in the regulation bridal T-shirt that proclaimed 'Team Brianna!' walked in. I was in the kitchen when I heard the cheer and came out into the main space. But when I saw who one of the women was, I stopped in my tracks. Because there, smile paused at half-beam when she saw me, was Maddie.

As I laid eyes on her, every muscle I had froze, and

all my blood stilled. The only thing moving was the expanding bubble of fear in my throat, threatening to rise up and choke me. Damn it, what the hell was she doing here in my workplace, my town? She had no right.

However, ever the consummate professional, I reminded myself this wasn't about me. This was about the bride and her day, and Helen who'd flung a ton of money our way to make this day special. I was going to make sure that happened. I'd done a drama class at uni, and now was the time to dip in and gather all those skills. I was going to need them, of that I was sure.

I stepped forward to greet them. "Welcome, ladies!" I checked my watch, before glancing back up, avoiding Maddie's stare at all costs. "You've got ten minutes to grab a pastry and a coffee, and then I hope you're ready to get cupcaking!" I gave them a broad grin and rubbed my hands together, ignoring the insistent thud of my heart in my chest.

The universe was clearly determined to play tricks on me today, and I had no idea why.

The three other newbies trooped past me, showing miles of white teeth and yards of glossy hair. Plus, they all smelled delicious. Women usually did. Walking around this space was like going into a perfume department, with everyone fresh and ready for the day. I knew that soon, those smells would be overtaken with the aromas of baking.

But it wasn't cake I was thinking about as Maddie

drew up beside me, a pained look on her face. "We meet again." She had the good grace to look awkward at least. "I know you told me you were into baking, but I didn't put two and two together."

"And I didn't expect you to turn up to a baking class." Maddie's culinary skills when we were together had extended to buttering toast.

She swept her gaze around the room, before turning it back to me. "I didn't have much choice. But this is impressive, Jus. You've even got branded aprons. I think you were underselling yourself when we last met."

"I wasn't trying to impress you." I swallowed down the lump in my throat.

"I know." Maddie glanced at me. Her cheekbones were still as angular as ever. People often thought Maddie could contour like a demon. They didn't know what I knew: that she just had naturally gorgeous cheekbones.

I took a deep breath. I had a class to teach and cakes to bake. Today, Maddie was just another baker. Nothing more.

Maddie's lips curled into an awkward smile.

Lips I'd tasted numerous times. Emotions long forgotten began to stir. I blinked, trying to erase my thoughts.

"I better get ready — we've got cakes to bake." I gave her a look. "Are you any good at baking these days?"

She quirked her mouth into that smile I used to love. I didn't go weak at the knees; it just took me back to a different time in my life. A time when things had felt far simpler.

"You do remember what a disaster I was in the kitchen?"

It was a question that didn't need an answer. "Things might have changed since then. I was hardly Mary Berry."

"But you enjoyed it, you were always creative. Let's just say me and my Just Eat app are on very good terms."

I put a hand on my hip. "Get yourself a coffee, get your apron on and prepare to get floury."

"It's my only mission today." She squeezed past me, her body rubbing up against mine in a way it really didn't need to. Or was that just my imagination? Whatever, a frisson of something scampered up my backbone and landed on top of my diaphragm, causing my mind to freeze and my body to shiver.

Maddie caught my eye and gave me a half-smile, her cheeks colouring. Had she felt it, too?

I glanced around the room. The trick to making today work was to keep Maddie and I as far apart as possible, and not to let on to Amisha that I'd not only slept with her, I'd given her nearly four years of my life. And it had all started because of that damn mouth.

Chapter Nine

Brianna's hen party was no different from any other: the floor was still covered in glitter. We'd just waved the bride and her party off to the pub, and Amisha had stepped out to get a birthday card for her mum before the shops shut.

I was wiping down one of the benches when a knock on the still-open front door made me look up.

Maddie. Wearing her show-stopping smile and looking pristine. As if she hadn't been working with flour for the past few hours.

"Hey." She walked over to me, her familiar long stride making something in my stomach wobble low down. Was it weird to remember the way she walked? Even ten years on, every facet of her was still tattooed on my soul. I smiled, although I was pretty sure it didn't reach my eyes. After a day of teaching, tiredness was curling around my bones.

"Can I help?"

I stopped wiping. "Shouldn't you be at the pub? You're on a hen weekend in case you hadn't noticed."

She shrugged. "They won't miss me for a while. They're

currently ordering porn star martinis and I know where that leads. I'll let them get a head start and I can catch up later. Plus, I wanted to come back and let you know I really enjoyed today. You're good at this. Not that I'm surprised. You always were a go-getter." She swept her hand through the air. "And this proves you've got it. Your own business. Impressive."

I decided to take her compliment at face value. "Thanks." I pointed at the aprons scattered around the benches. "If you want to help, you can gather up all those and put them in a pile by the door."

Maddie nodded, then did as she was told.

"How did you find the class? As someone who's not a baker? I'm always intrigued to know."

She looked up, her grey gaze settling on my face. It was strangely comforting and familiar. As if the intervening years had never happened. "You've got a very easy style that made it a snap for even a novice like me. Plus, you put humour into it, which always helps. The vagina cupcakes are going to live long in my memory and my taste buds. A vanilla-flavoured labia is the stuff of lesbian dreams."

I let out a snort of laughter. "I'm just catering to the crowd." As predicted, the vagina cupcakes served with prosecco had caused gales of laughter and a photo-storm. I still thought eating cupcakes with flowers on top was preferable to eating one with a vagina on it. Maybe that's why I was still single.

"If I have to do penis ones for straight hen parties, I decided I'd do vagina ones for lesbians. Plus, who doesn't want to lick their tongue through a buttercream vulva?"

As soon as it came out of my mouth, I gave myself a mental kick in the shins. The last thing I wanted to be accused of was flirting. I pulled my shoulders back and stood taller, as if reasserting my original intentions. I hoped it worked. The way Maddie's eyes were sparkling when I looked back at her, I wasn't sure it had. Or had they been lit up the whole time?

"I can't think of a better way to spend a Saturday afternoon."

I couldn't help but smile. I was proud of our business, and Maddie had pressed the right button. My Maddie resolve was softening like the President butter we used in our buttercream icing.

Maddie dumped the aprons by the door, then stood on the opposite side of the bench I was wiping down.

"You can put those cupcakes in the fridge if you want to make yourself useful." I indicated the boxes from today, which were still standing on the worktops. "They should still be good for you to collect when you've got a massive hangover tomorrow."

She shook her head as she walked towards them. "I hope they're not going to make me do shots."

I thought back to all the times I'd tried to make Maddie do shots at university. They were never her forte, and she'd always suffered the next morning. By around year three, she'd committed to avoiding shots, and all her friends knew the drill.

"How do you know the bride?"

She shut the fridge door and came to stand back near me. Her nearness caused the fair hairs on the back of my head to stand on end.

"It's complicated. I used to go out with her intended, but it was a long time ago and it wasn't for long."

I raised a delicate eyebrow. "You've shagged the other bride?"

"If it makes it any better, I don't actually recall doing it. You know those times when the sex was so drunken and so long ago, your memory does you a favour and scrubs it from your brain? Well, Amy was one of them."

"So what you're saying is Brianna's getting a drunken shag as a wife?" Poor Brianna, she seemed lovely.

"Not anymore. Amy has a drink problem, and now she doesn't touch a drop. Hence she's not here on this hen do; not really her scene. I imagine she's a fantastic sober shag, although I don't really like to think about it too much."

"Do you know any of the other women?"

She nodded. "They're a huge part of my past. I partied hard with most of them back in the day. All except Bri's mum, of course. It's good to see them, but hen parties aren't really my style." She paused. "Plus, I'm not such a party girl anymore. When I got settled in London, I stopped going out so much. And now I'm living here, I'm throwing myself into my work. I'd love to get a dog eventually and settle down."

I stared at her features, so familiar and yet so alien. When we meet people from our past, we often think we know them because we remember things. But I didn't know Maddie at all anymore. I knew she didn't like shots, but everything else might have changed. Tastes in food, films, politics, clothes. People were always morphing and changing, and Maddie was almost a stranger to me now.

Almost.

"Anything else I can do while you're clearing up?"

I cocked my head. "If you really want to help, you could take all the blades off the mixers and put them in the sink over there." I pointed towards the industrial-sized stainless steel sinks on the back wall. "Just make sure the mixers are unplugged. I wouldn't want to be responsible for any terrible injuries to your hands."

For the love of all things good, why the hell couldn't I think before I spoke?

Maddie widened her eyes at me. Then she leaned over the mixer to check it was unplugged. It was. When she looked up, she was smiling. "I thought you'd stopped caring about my hands a long time ago."

"I did. It's just that if you sue me, my insurance premiums will go through the roof."

She tipped her head back and let out a cackle. "Good one." She went to the next mixer, checked it was unplugged and removed the blades.

"You don't have to do this, you know."

She glanced up again. "I know, but there's only so much

hen partying I can take in one day, so this is a welcome respite. They're all talking about marriage and babies. It's seriously doing my head in." She paused. "But I loved what you did today. I'll be recommending you to all the other lesbians queueing up to get married at the moment. It's like an epidemic."

"You're not joining the queue?"

She gave a derisory laugh. "Not anytime soon, seeing as I'm single."

A frisson of something slid down me under Maddie's warm, insistent gaze.

"Since us, meaningful relationships haven't really been my forte."

My heartbeat slowed as I took in her words. "It's been years since we were together. I've no idea what you've been up to. Things might have changed."

"Some things don't, do they?" She cast her gaze to the floor, then back up. "You have in some ways — you've got this business. But you're still you. Still capable, gorgeous." She paused. "Still incredible brown eyes. I'm surprised someone hasn't talked you into having a hen party and put a ring on it."

I shook my head. She had some gall coming in here and saying that, when it was meant to have been her all those years ago. Or had she forgotten that?

"I'm concentrating on getting my business right. And you know what they say: you can't have it all. I've got a great business and home. My love life will sort itself out when the time's right. I learned a long time ago that if you focus on something you really want but can't have, it doesn't change anything." I looked her dead in the eye. "It was a harsh lesson. The best thing to do is to move on."

Right there in front of me, Maddie squirmed. Actually squirmed. I'd waited years to see that.

She took the mixer blades and dumped them in the wide sink at the back of the room, filling it with water and washing up liquid. It wasn't lost on me that we'd been chatting quite amiably, but our past was always lurking, wasn't it? Always waiting to catch us off guard when we least expected it.

"Still, I'm surprised you're single. You were a great girlfriend." She held up a hand as she paused and turned to me. "I was a great girlfriend for a while, and then I turned into the shittiest one on earth. You don't have to point that out, by the way. I know I had a habit of running."

Suddenly I recalled the other time Maddie had run. It wasn't just the time that ended everything. Maddie had gone AWOL once previously about a year into our relationship, too. She'd said then she just had "a wobble", and eventually, we'd settled back into being us. But as it turned out, it had been prophetic.

Maddie sighed. "But underneath this stony exterior, there's a tiny piece of me who's still a hopeless romantic. I'm just waiting for the right woman to come along and unlock it."

Her gaze rested on my face. For a second, it was just

the two of us, like before: Maddie and Justine, like always. Only, it was never going to be that again, was it?

I shook my head and busied myself stacking up some of the hen party's cake plates. Trying to ignore my racing pulse, the way my insides swayed when she looked at me. I wasn't going to build a new future on a look, was I?

"Maybe she'll come along when you least expect it. Maybe you'll meet her tonight. Maybe it'll be Brianna's mum, she seemed game."

Maddie snorted at that, her back to me again as she washed the blades. "I think sleeping with Brianna *and* her mum might be something even I wouldn't stoop to."

I stopped wiping down the bench as she finished rinsing. Then she dried her hands and walked over to the bench. I stared as she undid the next few mixer blades, and took them back to the sink.

"I thought you'd slept with the other bride."

Maddie gave an embarrassed shrug, not turning around. "One, two, who's counting. It was all a very long time ago. Just thinking about it now makes me tired."

I shook my head at her. "You were never a player when we were together, or before. What changed?"

She cleared her throat, drying her hands on a tea towel. A tell-tale rouge crept onto her cheeks. "I went a bit off the rails after I left you. Had a crazy few years." She shrugged, clutching the sink behind her. "It happens. They all take the piss out of me now as I'm so not who I was when I met them. I'm a lot calmer and wiser."

"You were the opposite of wise when you left me. You broke my heart and you broke the hearts of all our friends, too. It wasn't just me you left that day, you know."

We stared at each other for a long moment, before Maddie looked away. She walked over and unhooked another two blades, placing them in the sink. The sound reverberated around the room again. When she turned back, her gaze met mine. My insides melted a little, like fresh butter on hot toast.

"If it helps any, I agree. I was a fool, but I can't turn back time, can I?"

I shook my head. "You can't. We're both living very different lives now."

Maddie stared at me. "Very different, and yet, here we are. The two of us, chatting. Not so different, is it?" Then she dropped her head and began moving at speed, yanking the mixer blades off with far less finesse, avoiding eye contact.

Was it different? Yes, drastically. To me, anyway. Maddie might be back in my life, but she wasn't the one who mattered most. Not anymore.

The air in the room was far heavier now, and I wanted Maddie to leave. She was the one encroaching on my set-up, after all. She seemed to get the message as she washed the last blades, her hands and head down. For a few seconds, the only sound was running water and the clatter of blades in the sink. Then the taps shut off.

I turned and saw she held the property detail brochures Gemma had left out for me.

"Are you looking for new premises?"

I nodded. "We are. This space is small, and we're turning business away. We can't decide whether to open another site or move to a bigger one."

"A nice problem to have." She walked back towards me and picked up her bag. Her mouth opened and closed, then she shook her head almost imperceptibly.

"Were you going to say something?"

She glanced up at me, her eyes soft. She put her bag down. "Just that we might be running into each other a little more what with Kerry being pregnant." She paused. "Nothing's set in stone, is it? James and Kerry thought they had it all worked out; getting married, buying a house, even getting pregnant."

My heart dropped. I kept forgetting and then it kept coming back to me. Kerry was pregnant. Whatever it was that Maddie and I were doing now, it was nothing compared to that.

"She seemed pretty chipper when we were at her house, but she must go through patches of utter despair." I caught her gaze. "Was she surprised when she found out?"

Maddie nodded. "She was, although I think she'd primed herself. But thinking it might be and knowing for sure are two very different things. She needs some time off, to rest up. If anything happens to this baby… That would be like losing James all over again. Once is more than enough."

"Agreed." I shook my head. "Love is a fickle thing, and

even if you have it, it can be taken away at a moment's notice." I was talking about James dying, but Maddie put her focus on the floor again, before checking her watch. Maybe she was realising there were easier places to be than reminiscing with me.

"I better get going before they send a search party." She paused, biting her lip. "Could we do this again?"

"You want a private baking class? They cost a lot of money."

She sighed, and just in that second, the old Maddie was there. The one I used to love. And it took my breath away.

"I meant this. Us. Chatting. If I swung by one day, would you go for a coffee with me? Or maybe even a drink? Since I've been back, I keep driving past The Spanish Station and remembering all our times there."

Maddie and I had gone to The Spanish Station for a drink just after we'd started dating, and had spent a dreamy few hours chatting, kissing and laughing with each other. Our tapas had gone cold and we hadn't cared at all. Ever since, The Spanish Station had been *our* bar, a regular destination of old. Hence since we split, I hadn't been back. I frowned. A drink at The Spanish Station was loaded with memories. "I'm not sure why we'd do that."

"Because we're friends?"

"Are we?" I really wasn't as sure about that as Maddie seemed to be. "You've got your own life, and I've got mine. I bake and cook and read. You go on hen weekends and are the life and soul of the party."

"I already told you that's not true. Plus, you can be the life and soul when you want to be, too."

I ignored that. "I told you at the funeral. I'm happy to see you when we meet up as a group. But trying to go back and rekindle something you have vague memories of isn't going to work."

"My memories aren't vague."

"Mine are." But as I said it, I was holding the wooden bench, fearful that my body's reaction to the blatant lie might seep through my skin.

I remembered every inch of Maddie's body, every patch of her skin, and every inch of the miles of lies she'd told. Which is why, despite what my body was saying, I was sticking to my guns. If she wanted to get back together with everyone else, she could. But she didn't have to make a special case for me.

Still, she was giving me that look, the one I always was a sucker for. I swallowed and held my ground, literally and metaphorically.

"I'm not asking for a date. Just a coffee to catch up on old times and to see how your family are."

"You care about my family?"

"I care about you, and so by extension, yes, I care about your family." She paused. "But I know anything romantic is in the past. I'm not stupid." She tapped the workbench and then walked past me. As she reached the door, she looked over her shoulder. "Anyway, I better go. I'll see you around?"

I nodded. "You might."

"Have a great night."

I watched her leave, giving me a wave through the glass doors as she left. My past walking away from me once again, just like before. Only, it wasn't like before, was it? Because now I was in control of my destiny, and I was a strong, independent woman. I had the upper hand here, because I knew what Maddie wanted. She could give me those hangdog looks all day long; it wasn't going to work. I wasn't going to jump to her tune just because she'd come back.

I turned, and my eye snagged on something black: Maddie's bag. She'd left it, and I had no doubt she'd need it. I sprang into action, and shot out of the door, the early evening rays zapping the street as I stepped out. Maddie was already striding down the path, not looking back.

"Maddie!" My shout pierced the air, and up ahead, a couple walking a dog turned their heads.

Maddie turned, puzzlement creasing her face.

I held up her bag, trying to appear nonchalant. "Your bag!" In the bakery opposite, Rob gave me a wave, his blonde Viking beard shining under his store lights. His beard always looked like he'd baked it on himself.

I broke into a little jog towards Maddie, trying to multitask by waving back at Rob. Big mistake. I was clever in many ways, but never at multi-tasking. As I began to run, I stumbled on a loose stone, maybe a brick. I wasn't sure.

Alarm slithered through me as I tried to move my foot, but it wouldn't budge. Unlike the top half of my body, which was moving just fine.

Before I knew what was happening, I sailed through the warm air, and landed unceremoniously in a heap. Palms first, closely followed by my elbows, the sound of my bones crunching against the hard concrete loud in my ears. Pain skittered through me like a pinball. I gasped for breath as I took stock. I was sprawled on the pavement like one of those police procedure crime scenes. All I needed was someone to draw around me with a big hunk of chalk. Ta-da!

I lay there for what seemed like an eternity, trying to work out where it hurt the most. My hands, my knees, or my ego. It was a three-way tie.

When I looked up, Maddie was standing over me, her face pale, concerned and beautiful. Would I ever think she wasn't beautiful? I was beginning to think the odds were stacked against it.

"Are you okay?" She squatted beside me, and when I looked up, I got an eyeful of the smooth skin just below her neck. I hadn't noticed it earlier, but now it was up close, it was all I could see. When I lifted my gaze higher still, I found Maddie's eyes on me, soft, gentle, concerned. When our gazes locked, I shuddered.

Inside, I'd had my guard up. Now it was down, I was vulnerable. Maddie's eyes were the same mesmeric grey, and her lips were still inviting, just like always. Was it my imagination or were we moving closer, and were Maddie's eyes on my lips, too?

Maddie breathed in sharply. Then I felt other body heat

nearby, and the moment was broken. I wasn't sure whether I was relieved or sad.

"You okay, Jus?" Rob's deep voice barrelled through me as Maddie leaned back, her neck turning slightly pink. Rob's wrinkled brow came into sharper view. "I think you shook the bakery when you hit the pavement."

"Now's not the time to tell me I need to lose weight." I sat up, groaning as pain rippled through me. Had I torn my jeans? If I had, I could just chalk it up to fashion. I tried to ignore the emotion currently slaloming around my body, looking for an outlet but with nowhere to go.

"Your sense of humour's still intact, so that's a relief." He grinned at me, then turned to Maddie.

Imperceptible to the untrained eye, Maddie stole a glance at me, then slipped on her professional face. But I saw it. I lifted my arm slowly.

"Be careful, you might have broken something." Maddie touched my wrist.

"Mainly my pride, but I'll survive."

Maddie sat back on her haunches, glancing at Rob. "So this is the famous bakery you were telling me about at the funeral. I didn't realise it was *right* here."

Rob nodded. "Right opposite Justine and Gemma. Which means I get to see her falling on her arse whenever the moment takes her."

I glanced up at them, laughing over my pain. "When you two have quite finished, can one of you help me up?"

They both stood up, then Maddie held out a hand,

with me wincing and groaning throughout. If I was trying to act cool and calm around Maddie, I'd just blown my cover.

She gave me a smile, her arm around my waist. Her hand rested on my hip bone, and my body warmed to it, leaned into it. Until I remembered who it belonged to and why that wasn't allowed. I went to move away, then winced. Pain shot up from my kneecap and I doubled over.

Maddie's arm tightened around me and happy endorphins pinged around my body, duelling with the pain currently crashing through it. A vision of Maddie sitting in the front row of my funeral sailed across my mind and I rolled my eyes at myself. That wasn't going to happen; and even if it did, my romantic fantasies really needed work. If my fantasies involved me dead, my fantasies needed an upgrade.

When I glanced back up, Maddie's stare hadn't moved. If eye fucking really was a thing, as Gemma had told me recently, we were doing it.

"Thanks for running after me." She reached down and picked up her bag, but her eyes had dropped to my lips. "I'd never have heard the end of it if I'd turned up minus my bag, and so minus my wallet."

"Glad to be of service." If anyone were to run a heat map over my body, it would be red at my core. Our gazes connected again, and the moment stilled, before breaking into tiny, invisible shards. Maddie slung the bag over her shoulder. She had broad shoulders. Strong. I dragged my eyes away.

"Anyway," she said. "I don't like leaving you here, injured. But I really should get to the pub." She winced.

"Absolutely. You've got a hen party to do."

"Will you make sure she's okay?" Maddie said to Rob.

He nodded. "Of course. She's in safe hands." He flashed his palms to demonstrate their suitability.

Maddie took a deep breath, then nodded. "Okay. Try not to fall over too much in the meantime." She took my hand in hers, turning it upwards. "Make sure you clean these up. Your hands are important." She glanced up and our gazes locked one more time. My heart boomed. It was all getting a bit intense. Then, with a soft nod and a smile that danced in my vision for moments after, she walked away.

Her smile took me right back to our old life. Standing graduating together, with the whole world before us and so much to look forward to.

Before it had all crumbled into dust.

I stared after her, transfixed and confused. What the fuck did she do to me?

"Will you live or should I call an ambulance?" Rob put his hands on my shoulders. "Do you need an emergency pastry to ease the pain?" He knew they were my weak spot.

"I always need a pastry." I gave him a smile, even though my whole body had just turned up its throbbing. "Thanks for dashing to my rescue."

He flicked his eyes towards Maddie, who was just turning the corner. "You fell hard, but I don't think I was really needed." He paused. "So I take it things have thawed a little between you since the funeral?"

I shrugged like it meant nothing. "She turned up in my cupcake class today, so necessity lent a hand."

Rob put an arm around my shoulder and guided me into the bakery, sitting me on a stool while he went behind the counter. "Just necessity? Nothing else?"

I shook my head. "No, nothing else. That ship sailed a while ago. You remember the ship's name, right? The Titanic?"

He stilled and raised a single eyebrow in my direction. "What's that look for?"

"Me thinks the lady doth protest too much." He grabbed a pastry with his tongs, and put it on a plate. "I got the impression I was crashing a party for two when I rocked up."

I shook my head. "You weren't." My insides were twirling like a majorette's baton, round and round and round. "You have an over-active imagination. You thought there was something between me and the new postie last month, remember?"

Rob scooted around the counter, bringing me my pastry. "In my defence, she did bring you three parcels in one day. If that's not love, I don't know what is." He paused. "But this was more than the postie. I felt it. Didn't you?"

I shook my head. "No. I felt the pavement, but that's all." That's all I was prepared to concede, at any rate.

He narrowed his eyes. "If you say so. Now, shall I make a coffee to go with that?"

Maddie's smile flashed into my vision. I closed my eyes, shaking it from my head. "Yes, please."

Chapter Ten

My parents lived in Montpelier, now considered one of the more arty areas of Bristol. When we were growing up, though, it hadn't been the case. But now, they were living among the artists and the styled street art, which Mum was weirdly proud of. I loved their house, a quirky semi-detached cottage with white brickwork walls inside and far more light and space than you'd first think from the outside. I was visiting today at the behest of my mother, who'd ordered me around for lunch because, "I've almost forgotten what my only daughter looks like". She could never say that about my brother Dean, who only lived streets away and still brought his washing home for her to do.

After yesterday, I was glad I'd agreed, because a home-made Sunday lunch always soothed my soul.

Mum was washing up when I walked into the house via the back door, straight into the kitchen. I put the cupcakes I'd made yesterday on the side in their pristine white cake box, then kissed the back of Mum's head and flicked the kettle on. "Hey, Mother Dearest."

She turned her head before she replied. "Is it really you or is it a mirage?"

"It's really me." I opened the biscuit tin and plucked a shortbread out. They were pleasingly fat and left tell-tale grease on my fingers.

"Are there cakes in that good-looking box?"

"There are," I replied. "Cupcakes from yesterday. You'll be pleased to know they're decorated with flowers and shapes, too, and not vaginas."

She laughed out loud. "Another hen party or were you just in the mood?"

"You know my feelings, definitely a hen party." I popped the last of the shortbread in my mouth. "Where's Dad?" I couldn't see him when I peered into the lounge. His end of the sofa was unoccupied.

"Still at the pub. He's got a football thing today." Dad was a big Bristol City fan and was secretary of the fan club. He quite often had a 'football thing', which my brother and I had always decided was code for 'a need to be down the pub drinking beer without his family'. It was an impulse I well understood now I was older. My brother and I still referred to the need for a drink as 'a football thing'.

"Did we win yesterday?" I normally kept up with the scores, but yesterday had been my most bizarre Saturday in quite a while. The affairs of Bristol City hadn't been high on my agenda.

Mum turned, her face looking like she'd just swallowed a fly. "Draw. 3-3. Last-minute equaliser by them."

Now it was my turn to mirror her face. Dad was a gentle man, but football had always dictated his mood. Win, and he was happy all weekend; but if City lost, as they frequently did, he was always grumpy for a few hours, sometimes all weekend. A draw could see it go either way.

My mum could never understand it. As she said, by the law of averages, you were going to win some and lose some. But Dad never went into it like that. He was the eternal optimist and always expected City to win. It was amazing he wasn't a crushed soul after 60 years of support.

"Let's hope he's had a good time at the pub today."

"He's fine. Even getting quite stoic about. Yesterday at dinner, he said, and I quote, 'You win some, you lose some'."

"He did not."

"He did." Mum wiped her hands on the tea towel neatly folded on the oven door handle, before grabbing me by the shoulders.

I stood to attention as if I was in the army.

"Let me get a proper look at you." She did just that. "You're looking well. I like your hair like that. Have you highlighted it?"

I shook my head. "Nope. Just been getting out in the sun. I think it's gone a shade lighter." My hair was what hairdressers called 'fair'. Less kind folks called it 'mousy'.

"Were you working yesterday?"

I nodded as she let me go and made the tea. "Class of 14 learning how to make cupcakes. A lesbian hen party."

That made her turn her head. "Lesbians baking? That's not much of a surprise. You and Gemma run it, after all. Did you know anybody?"

I cleared my throat. "I did." I paused. "Maddie was in the class."

Mum turned to me fully when I said that. "Maddie? Your Maddie?"

"There's only one Maddie." Not strictly true. I'm sure there were umpteen Maddies all over the world, but only one had played a key role in my life so far.

"There's only one Maddie I'd like to kick from here to kingdom come. What was she doing there?"

"She was part of the hen party." I rolled my neck to show how relaxed I was about Maddie's reappearance. "I saw her at James's funeral, too. So it seems the universe has decided now is our time to meet up again."

Mum drew her lips in a tight, straight line. "I know it was a long time ago, but I still remember the hurt she caused. No trips down memory lane, okay?"

"It's fine, I'm a big girl now. I saw her, spoke to her and didn't expect to see her again. And then, she turned up again yesterday. She's a crap baker, that much I know. But apart from that, her life and my life have been separate for a very long time, and I don't see a reason to change that." I paused. "You're not the only one who remembers all the hurt."

Mum nodded, satisfied for now. "Good." She picked up the tea. "Shall we take this through?"

My parents' lounge was L-shaped and had a feature log burner in the fireplace, which lay dormant on this summer afternoon. At just after 1:00 pm, the sunshine was splashed in blocks up the lounge wall like a particularly seasonal Rothko painting. I settled on the two-seater tan settee with its well-worn leather. Mum's much-loved antique patterned rugs covered bare, polished floorboards underfoot.

My parents weren't style gurus, but they were definitely far more stylish than most parents I knew. I wasn't sure where Mum got her eye from, as nothing in her background screamed design. She might work at Marks & Spencer's, but her downtime was filled with interior design, and watching makeover shows on TV. 'Elle Décor' and other such magazines littered the coffee table and were stacked in a pile by the settee. My house had similar piles, but of baking and cooking magazines.

"So what's madam up to these days?"

If Mum didn't trust a woman, she was always called 'madam'. Like she was a specialist hooker.

"She's a property developer, and doing pretty well for herself reading between the lines. In any case, she looks good." I still remembered our locked gaze after I fell. I could still feel it like a separate heartbeat in my soul. "She was living in London, but there was an opportunity here, so she switched her focus and moved back. She knows the area, so it made sense."

Mum took a sip of her tea before replying. "You seem to know a lot about her."

"I told you, I saw her at the funeral and she wanted to chat to me. She apologised for how things ended all those years ago."

"So she bloody well should."

I loved it when Mum got all protective. "I can't change the past, but I can control the future. So stop looking so worried. I might see a little more of her now everyone is back in touch, but she's going to have to do more than just show up and expect everybody to fall into place."

"What did everyone else say?"

"Gemma was ready to punch her for me, I just had to give the signal." I shrugged. "But I can handle it."

Mum raised an eyebrow. "I hope you're right."

The front door slamming signalled that someone was home, and moments later my brother Dean popped his head around the corner. When he saw me, his eyes lit up. Ever since we were little, Dean had always been thrilled to see me. When it came to his family, he was like a dog, his tail always wagging and perky.

"Justine!" Dean always said my name in two very distinct syllables, the first part lower in tone, the second almost sung. If my brother had a volume control, I'd never found it and no matter how many times he did it in public, I never got used to it. He scooped me up in a hug, before doing the same to Mum, then sitting down. "I didn't know you were coming. No baking today?"

"Nope. Everyone deserves a day off."

Dean licked his lips. "Any more vagina cupcakes?"

"She ate them all yesterday." Mum guffawed at her own joke, followed by my brother. My family humour was strange sometimes. I ignored Mum and turned to my brother.

"So how's your work going? Last time I saw you, that project you were working on was coming to a close." Dean was a builder and had been working with the same developer on a massive project for the past year. Now that was coming to an end and a couple of planned jobs had fallen through, he'd been getting a little antsy. I was sure it would work out for him as good builders were hard to come by, but he wasn't so calm.

"Still a bit up in the air. I've got a few irons in the fire and I've got money saved up, but I'd like a project to really sink my teeth into."

"I'm sure something will come up." Mum's response was the same every time, and Dean gave me a look as she said it.

"Where's Dad?"

"He's got a football thing at the pub," Mum replied.

Another knowing look to Dean, and we both suppressed a laugh. He'd driven me nuts when we were growing up, but now I was pretty happy to have my younger brother in my corner as an ally, especially as our parents were approaching retirement age. Some of my friends were only children and all the responsibility fell to them. Plus, who did they make faces at when their parents said stupid things?

"If you're at a loose end, you could always come around to mine and do those jobs you promised you would do when you had some free time." Dean had been telling me he was going to fix my slightly off-kilter bedroom doors for the past year, as well as fixing a couple of wonky cupboards in my kitchen. Even though I rented, it was at mate's rates from a friend, so I was happy to do a few odd jobs without bothering her.

"What'll you do for me in return?"

"Not give you a wedgie?"

Dean's laugh reverberated around the lounge. "You couldn't give me a wedgie now if you tried. I'm far too big and strong."

"But I'm light and agile, you seem to forget. That trumps it all. Low centre of gravity. Like that new forward for Bristol City." I sat back, a grin on my face. Although the bruises on my knees and elbows told a different story, but my family didn't know that, did they?

"When you two have quite finished your plans to beat each other up," Mum said. "Dean, go fix things for your sister. Justine, bake a cake for your brother in return."

We both grinned at each other. Instructions from on high.

"Next week any good? I'll come around and see the extent of the damage. So long as you don't mind a bit of mess in your life?"

I thought about the last few weeks. "My life's messier than you might care to imagine, so what's a bit of dust between family?"

"There's a joke there about the dust settling, but I can't

quite pin it down." He leaned over and patted my knee. "You can tell me all about it next week." He turned to Mum. "What's for lunch?"

"Roast chicken."

"My favourite!" both Dean and I chorused.

Mum rolled her eyes. "I know."

Chapter Eleven

"I'm going to miss you if you move." Rob stood on the step of The Bristol Bakery, locking up. It was another hot mid-July day, the sun cutting the path with a yellow stripe. "Are you looking in Bristol and Bath, or just here?"

"Both." I fell into step beside him, both of us walking to my car. Rob's was in the garage and I was giving him a lift home. Rob was one of the many reasons not to leave, but with Kerry's money now firmly in our sights, it seemed like it was written in the stars. Rob was the one who'd told Gemma and I about our current location, having already opened his bakery two years earlier. It'd been fantastic working so closely with an old friend, and I'd miss him, too.

"I'd like to stay in Bristol just to keep it real, plus the transport links are better with the airport nearby. But if something comes up in Bath, we'd take it. Bath is just as good for baking."

Rob nodded. "It is. Bath is a chocolate box town and you make a slice of chocolate box every day. It suits it perfectly." He sighed. "But wherever you end up, I won't have anyone to chat to across the street, and that will make me very sad."

I bumped him with my hip. "I'm not gone yet, and we'll still see each other, won't we? Nights out, dinner, drinks. You might even finally make it over to my place so I can repay that gorgeous dinner you cooked for me and Gemma last month."

"Don't go making promises you can't keep."

"Besides, whoever takes over might be much nicer and then you'll never need to see us again."

He laughed. "When you put it like that."

I gave him a look. "Life changes, at least that's what Gemma keeps telling me. And apparently, change is good. Change drives you forward."

Rob gave me a look that told me he didn't believe a word as we got into Kermit. The inside was salamander-grill hot, so I put the air-con on straight away. When I touched the steering wheel, I swore. It almost singed the tips of my fingers.

"She's probably right, but I hate that self-help twaddle," he said, relaxing into his seat. "Although Jeremy is getting into meditating and wants me to do it, too. I keep telling him I can't, because it gives me the willies."

"As a gay man, is that not a good thing?"

He moved his sun visor down as I pulled out. The car hopped before settling down. Sometimes it really did think it was a frog.

"It's not. Being so still and contemplative reminds me of praying, and that reminds me of growing up in the cult that is the Catholic Church. And then my mind shuts down and I can't do it. So meditating isn't for me at all."

I laughed. "Is meditation even a possibility when you have two babies in the house?"

He chuckled. "My point exactly. But Jeremy says having two babies makes it even more imperative. I do wonder where he manages to fit it in, in between caring for the kids and running his business, but he does. He's a wonder of modern science. Which is why I put a ring on it as soon as I could."

Rob and Jeremy lived in the centre of Bath, not far from where Maddie was doing up her flat. Rob loved living in Bath and working in Bristol, saying it gave him the best of both worlds. Bristol was a more vibrant, buzzy city, whereas Bath was more old-school style and glamour. Bristol was Emma Stone, whereas Bath was Audrey Hepburn. I loved them both, but had to admit moving the business to Bath would make my current commute far easier, and would probably tempt more of the London crowd in, too.

"Have you seen Maddie recently?"

My cheeks heated at the memory of me falling on my arse. "Negative." I clutched the steering wheel that little bit tighter as we navigated the city centre. As we drove past Wapping Wharf, I glanced towards The Spanish Station. Our bar. After our first night there, we'd gone home and made love all night long, and Maddie had stared at me in the same way she'd stared at me after I fell on the path. Like she wanted me. When Rob said he'd felt something between us, I had, too. I hadn't known exactly what until this very moment.

"And are you sad you haven't seen her?"

Rob's gaze was heating me up again, just as the air-con was cooling me down. "Nope. We're ancient history, so it's fine."

He let a few beats go by before he spoke again. "She's living in Bath, isn't she?"

We pulled up at some lights. "Kinda. She's doing up a flat around the corner from you."

"So I might see her in Chequers?" That was Rob's much-beloved local.

"You might. Maybe you can become best friends with her."

He spluttered. "Not if I want you to talk to me again."

"Didn't stop James." I shook my head. "Anyway, that doesn't matter. What's done is done." I paused. "But we were something once, Maddie and I. Her coming back into my life has thrown me."

"I can tell."

Something fluttered in my chest. "She was going to be my Jeremy, my bench-warmer, you know?"

He gave me a puzzled look.

I smiled. "At my funeral. She was going to be the chief mourner, the one on the front bench. Our whole life was mapped out, but she tore it up. So seeing her again is tinged with fear. A bit of grieving for what I lost, and a bit of futility because I still don't know why. Oh, she tried to explain, but..." I shook my head.

"Maybe you should ask her again. Maybe there's still a chance."

"Just because you're in the perfect relationship, stop trying to put your relationship goals onto me."

Rob's laugh filled the car. "Does anyone have a perfect relationship? Damn sure ours isn't. It's held together by Jeremy's patience and child-rearing, and my culinary and cleaning prowess. Otherwise, we'd have killed each other by now."

Jeremy ran his online stationery business from their spare room while also caring for the twins. Consequently, his life-management skills were second to none.

"If your relationship isn't perfect, there's no hope for any of us." I focused on the road, thinking about Maddie. About what she'd said when she spoke about waiting for the right woman to come along. Had I been waiting, too?

"And Justine?"

I glanced left. "Yeah?"

"If you died tomorrow, there would be a queue of people to sit on the front bench, so you don't have to worry. And I'd be first in the queue."

Chapter Twelve

I couldn't believe it was nearing the end of July already. After the first half of the year had crawled by as we watched our friend die, the second half was flying past at speed. We'd just waved a class off, the end of five days of learning how to bake and decorate a cake to a high standard. The class had the normal mix of women wanting to shake up their lives, and they'd all left with some amazing cakes and new-found confidence.

As usual, after five days of teaching I was exhausted. On my horizon I saw a bottle of Rioja and a Chinese. That is, until I remembered my brother was due in a minute to come home with me and measure up for his side of the sibling bargain. It had only taken him three weeks.

Gemma appeared from the back, typing something into her phone as she walked. She finished and looked up, her eyes sweeping the scene of devastation. Mixing bowls, nozzles, cutters, tools, boards — all dirty. I loved the tools of baking, but I didn't love washing them up. Luckily, today it wasn't my job. After months of trying different cleaners, we'd finally found a reliable one and she was due in 15 minutes. After just two weeks, we were already wondering how we'd survived without her.

"What you doing now? Fancy a quick drink and we can look over these property brochures?" She picked them up and waved them in my face.

"I can't. Dean's coming and we're going back to mine to measure up for my cupboards."

"Dean's finally doing those?" My wonky cupboards had been a running joke for a while, but even the joke had died it'd been so long.

"Apparently." As if on cue, Dean turned up at the door. Instead of knocking, he squashed his face against the glass door as hard as he could, making us both smile. Brothers.

Gemma unlocked it and Dean gave her a hug.

"I'm trying to persuade Justine to come to the pub and look at property brochures." She untangled herself from him. "Could you be persuaded to come to the pub first?"

"I can always be persuaded to have a pint," Dean replied.

I folded my arms across my chest and sighed at Gemma. "Is this because you want me to say yes to a new premises, so you're going to ply me with booze?"

Gemma tilted her head. "We've got money, but you're still dragging your heels. So yes, you could do with a nudge. Plus, we could get Dean's professional opinion, seeing as he'll be involved."

"I will?"

"Yes, you nugget," I replied. "If we need a builder, we're going to hire you."

"You better book me in then, before I get snapped up." Dean picked up a spatula and I could see he was contemplating licking it.

"Put it down." My voice was direct, as if I was talking to a dog. Dean put it down. "I thought you were nearly jobless?"

"Now I am, but things could change." He paused, looking around the room. "More to the point, if I can't lick the leftovers, is there any cake going spare?"

Gemma laughed, then walked over to the fridge, got a cake out and cut a slice for Dean

A knock on the door made us all look up.

Maddie.

I frowned, feeling my heart-rate tick up. What the hell was she doing here? It was hardly somewhere you just happened to be walking past. I went over and opened the door. Where the air in the room had been relaxed and convivial, now a cold blast of tension settled on us.

Maddie gave us a tight smile as she entered, nodding at Gemma, then at Dean.

Dean's face was a picture. Over Sunday lunch, he'd heard a little about Maddie being back on the scene, but I'd glossed over it. He hadn't seen her since he was 20, and he'd loved her back then.

"Hi again, Gemma. And hi, Dean. You're looking well."

Maddie cleared her throat. "How've you been?" That was directed at my brother.

Dean nodded. "Good. You?" Well, this was weird. Dean used to not-so-secretly fancy Maddie, so much so that Mum had to take the then-teenage Dean aside and tell him it wasn't such a great look to be mooning over his sister's girlfriend. He'd sulked for months when she left. He ought to try being me.

"Awesome," Maddie replied. "Anyway, to stop this turning into an especially awkward episode of a yet-to-be-filmed Larry David sitcom, I was just thinking of you today when I was looking at some auction brochures. There's one on in two weeks, and there are a couple of properties that you and Gemma might want to look at." She fished the brochure out of the leather bag hanging from her shoulder. The same one she'd left here after the cupcake class. "I wasn't sure if it was useful, but I thought I'd let you know anyway. I'll be going to the auction, so if you wanted to come along with an experienced bidder, that would be me." She prodded her chest with her index finger as she said the last part.

I glanced at Gemma, who was giving Maddie a blank stare.

Maddie moved back towards the door and stuck her head out, then back in again. "Just checking for traffic wardens or tow trucks after what you told the hen party."

She stood on the precipice, one foot in the door, one foot out. How poignant.

"We were just going to the pub to look at some brochures, so I guess you could come along too?" It was out of my mouth before my brain kicked into gear. Was that what I wanted to say? I had no idea. The amused look Gemma was giving me told me she wasn't sure if that was what I'd wanted to say, either.

"Sure," Maddie replied, putting the brochures back in her bag. "So long as I'm not intruding? I was just going to drop them off so you could have a think about it."

"It's no big deal. We're going to the pub near Justine's place. Yes or no, up to you." That was Gemma and she was using her clipped tone. Letting Maddie know this wasn't about her and she could fall into our plans or not. It was up to her. In that moment, I loved my best friend fiercely.

Maddie glanced at me, then at Gemma, then gave a short nod of her head. "If you're sure, then count me in." She paused. "My business partner Ally is in the shop next door. I'll just need to go and tell her. Be back in two minutes?"

I nodded. "Sure."

Maddie gave me a grin, then left the shop.

Gemma let the door close before she turned to me, a single eyebrow raised. "You know, for someone who didn't want Maddie back in your life, you just did a startling impression of exactly the opposite."

Chapter Thirteen

An hour later, we were all sitting in my local around a gnarled wooden table. We'd only been there for 20 minutes, but already I could see Dean falling back under Maddie's spell, and I wondered if she had some strange power over the Thomas family. My parents had loved her, too, until she upped and left. My dad would probably be eating out of the palm of her hand just like Dean within minutes of meeting her again. Men were easier to impress. My mum, however, would be a harder nut to crack.

Dean wasn't the only one laughing at someone's jokes. Maddie's business partner Ally had come along to the pub as she lived close by, and Gemma was now fluttering her eyelashes in her direction and generally being as subtle as a sledgehammer. It wasn't just one way, though. Ally was doing it right back.

I could see the appeal. I'd only met her for half an hour, but Ally was a whirlwind, one of those people who drew you in and made you want to know more. She was short and wiry, and she dripped charisma. Her short, dark hair framed her face like a lightning bolt and her skin was smooth and bronzed. Between Gemma being charming and Dean dissolving into a puddle of goo, I felt like a bit of a spare part. A fifth wheel in this double date.

"So how long have you two been working together?" Gemma asked, pulling us all into the conversation. She was sitting up a little too attentively waiting for Ally's answer. It made me want to laugh, but I couldn't burst her bubble. I'd seen this practised move from Gemma before.

"We met in an auction room, didn't we?" Ally's voice was gravelly and still true to her northern roots, her vowels punchy and consonants spiked. "I went in looking to buy a flat or a house, and I came out with that and a Maddie."

"I wasn't for sale, I might add," Maddie said. "But yes, we had coffee and it changed our lives. You don't get that many women bidding at auctions, and we'd seen each other around. When we met, we got on. When we realised we were both gay, it bonded us that little bit more."

"We've been business partners for just over two years." Ally took a slug of her gin and tonic. "And I have to say, I'm loving living here. It's a refreshing change from London. Plus, we've got a few projects on the go. Some going well, some not so well."

"Why's that?" Dean asked.

"The council," Maddie replied. "Getting planning permission is the bane of our lives. Especially when the building is Grade I listed, like the one in the Royal Crescent. We only want to move a wall, but you'd think we were asking to demolish it and start again. But anyway, I'm not going to moan."

"If she does moan, I've told her she's got to do it in a West Country accent." Ally tried to put one on for her next sentence. "I've been trying to perfect mine, but it's hard with such a strong northern one already."

"As you can hear, she's rubbish." Maddie laughed. "Accents are not your forte."

"Luckily, interior design and knocking down walls are." Ally grinned.

"I love a woman with a sledgehammer," Dean told her. "Nothing sexier."

"I agree." Ally turned to Gemma. "Ever wielded a sledgehammer? I think it would look good on you."

Gemma's cheeks blushed bright red. "Not really, I'm more likely to wield a spatula or a piping bag than a sledgehammer."

"Equally sexy," Ally replied. "Everyone needs cake in their lives, don't they?"

"So what do you think about those properties?" Maddie interrupted Ally and Gemma's blatant flirting to bring the conversation back to why we were all there. "This one especially could be great." She pointed her finger to the brochure Gemma had been nodding at a few minutes earlier. "You could have two workshops for your classes, and plenty of space for an office each, too. Plus, it's nice and near the train station, so great for people coming in for classes. Do people come from all over?"

I nodded. "They do. The furthest we've had was from Brazil, and she came for a week-long class. We get people coming from Europe regularly, so being close to the station is ideal."

"Not that far from the airport, either," Gemma added. "Which is what we ideally wanted."

"And would you be involved in the building work?" Maddie directed the question to Dean.

"If they book me, I will come. But you better book me quick. And I need paying in cash, not just cake."

"What about a cake in the shape of cash?" I asked.

"So long as there's cash in the middle of it," Dean replied, deadpan.

Maddie furrowed her brow. "Did you say you were at a loose end at the moment?"

Dean nodded. "Just waiting on a couple of bids to come back."

"We might have some work coming up if you're interested?" She looked at me. "If it's okay to give your brother some work?"

I nodded. What could I say? I wasn't sure if it was or it wasn't, but Maddie appeared to be seeping back into my life before my very eyes and I was powerless to stop it. The weird thing was that I felt fine about it, too. Being in this pub with her was fine. Dean laughing with her was fine. Gemma flirting with her mate was fine.

But why the hell was it all so fine? That's what I couldn't figure out. I decided to push those thoughts aside, for now.

"If Dean needs the work and you need a builder, I'm not going to get in your way."

Maddie studied my face, before giving me a nod. "That's fantastic news. Dean, consider yourself hired." She sat back shaking her head. "Who would have thought I'd be hiring Justine's little brother after all these years?"

"Not me," I replied.

* * *

After a couple of drinks, Dean, Ally and Gemma went for a Thai meal. We waved the trio off to the gorgeous cafe around the corner, me giving Gemma an inquisitive look and her skilfully ignoring it. Did Dean know he might be crashing a semi first date? Probably not. And even if he did, he'd still be delighted to be going to dinner with two women. My brother never was very quick on the uptake.

Maddie had to go back to Bristol.

I frowned. "You drove half an hour this way, only to have to drive back again now?"

She shrugged, not quite meeting my eye. "It was worth it, I had a good time. Plus, I'll probably stay over at the house tonight. I'll walk you home, seeing as my car's parked there." Maddie pulled on her lightweight bomber jacket as she spoke.

"Sure."

She fell into step beside me, her footsteps echoing mine perfectly. Dusk was just settling, but the air still gave us a warm hug. A bus drove past on the main road, its diesel engine splintering the silence. We walked past the Post Office, the florist and the local car repair garage before Maddie spoke.

"So what do you think about the premises? Could be a go?"

"It could, but it's a lot of work. I've always favoured going with something that was already done, but Gemma's more into getting a space we can mould to be our own. That scares me, but ultimately, it could make our business better. At least, that's what she keeps telling me."

"She's right. If you make it what you want, that's far better than working around what's there. You can make it to your exact specifications, right down to how many plug points you need and their exact position. All important when you need to plug in 20 mixers at a time, I assume."

I turned my head, taking in Maddie's outline as she walked. She was still attractive, there was no denying that. But discovering this new side to her was making her that little bit more attractive. She was taking an interest in our business, wanting to help, and making me see how change could be a positive step.

Gemma would be thrilled. As my business partner kept telling me, I could keep the old business running while she worked on the new one. Maybe it could work with Dean on-board and Maddie to bounce ideas off. It was certainly sparking ideas in my head.

"I know, and it's not something Gemma hasn't said

to me a million times before. Maybe we're too close now, though. Maybe I need an outsider to come in and show me the possibilities." I stopped. "Who knew that outsider would be you?"

She gave me a smile that warmed my toes.

"Not me." Maddie cleared her throat. "I'd love to buy you dinner one day. Just to catch up and chat about your business. My treat, it's the least I can do after everything."

My heart boomed at her words, but my feet dragged. The push and pull made my blood pulse, and my face told the story.

She held up her hands. "Just dinner, nothing more."

I waved my hand as we turned into my street, with its uniform rows of two-up, two-down terraces. Mine had an olive green front door I'd spent hours deliberating over. That was another reason why I didn't want to be involved in design decisions. I'd been known to take hours deciding what to eat in a restaurant, never mind what colour to put on the walls in our prospective new business.

"I don't think going out for dinner is a good idea, do you?" I paused, looking in her eyes. "But I'd love some help for our business if that's still on offer?"

Maddie was nodding her head before I'd finished my sentence. "Of course, I'm not mercenary. I'm doing this to help an old friend, which is what you and Gemma both are."

I smiled. "Pleased to hear it."

"If it makes you feel better, I'd ask Gemma out for

dinner, but I might be stepping on Ally's toes if the looks they were giving each other tonight are anything to go by."

"You noticed that, too?"

Maddie raised one of her perfect eyebrows. "Everyone but Dean."

Our laughter melted into one.

"It really was great to see you. Let me know about the auction. I'm going to bid on a couple of properties, but if you want to come too — even just to get a feel for it, not even to buy anything yet — then let me know, okay?"

She fished in her pocket and pulled out a business card, pressing it into my hand. "I know you can probably find me on social media, but that's got my number and email on it." She raised her soft grey gaze to me, the colour of gathering storms. "Even if we're not going to dinner, I'm pleased to be back in your life in whatever capacity. Get in touch if you want to come along, okay?"

I nodded, unable to think of a retort as a wave of emotion swept down me. Nothing was going to happen, and yet, something already was, wasn't it?

"See you soon, Justine." Her gaze was trained on me as she spoke, and then she leaned closer, her lips moving towards me, landing on my cheek and pressing lightly.

I stopped breathing. Just the fact of her lips so close to mine rendered me speechless.

Chapter Fourteen

It was ten weeks since her husband's funeral, and Kerry was on summer break. Against the advice of many, she'd gone back to work pretty soon after James's death, saying she wanted to be there for her classes before they took their GCSEs. Kerry was a natural teacher, her subjects being maths and drama. I hadn't been sure it was wise, but Kerry said work had been a lifeline, a bit of normality in her topsy-turvy world.

Today, she was in the neighbourhood of Cake Heaven, visiting a baby shop she'd been recommended. She'd called to see if I could meet for lunch. As it happened, today I had a class-free day, so I could. Although as Gemma always joked, every day was class-free for us, to which I always rolled my eyes. If we moved our business, my teaching days would go up for a while, as we expanded our offerings and needed people to teach. But I wanted to transition to no teaching in the long run. My plan was to run the operation, leaving Gemma and our freelance team of bakers to do the teaching. Operations and business development was where I wanted to be.

When Kerry approached, I gave her the biggest hug I could muster over her bump, which was finally starting to show at nearly six months. Gemma and I had been over to Kerry's house as much as she could fit us in since the funeral, and we were also in constant contact via WhatsApp.

"I'm not going to tell you how much bigger you are than two weeks ago, even though you are." I gave her a wide grin. "How are things?"

She gave me a tired smile. Her skin was pale, and she didn't look like she'd been sleeping. "The baby kicked last night for the first time, and I lay there, just willing James to be by my side." She closed her eyes. She was trying not to cry.

I took her hand and squeezed it.

She squeezed right back. "But he's not coming back, is he? Sometimes I forget and it totally knocks the wind from my sails." She tensed, then exhaled. "I'm trying to grieve naturally, but not too much because I can't upset the baby." She shook her head. "Other than that, life's ticking along. My family have been around making sure I don't top myself, and James's family are still stunned by the baby news."

"How are they doing?" James had been an only child, and his parents were still raw with grief.

"His mum is ringing all the time, telling me to rest up. But we're over the worrying period now, and I didn't even know I was pregnant during the first three months. I reckon if this baby can survive his father dying and stay alive, he's got a good chance of surviving the rest of the way, hasn't he?" She cradled her belly with her left palm. "Doesn't mean I'm not petrified. Can I do this without James by my side?"

I pulled her into another embrace, and her hair tickled my cheek. "You'll do just fine. And you're not on your own. You've got loads of support."

We had a coffee before we hit the store, nattily named Baby Gaga. From the look on Kerry's face, I could tell she wanted to buy the shop. She could certainly afford it. She'd already told me she wanted this baby to have it all. I imagined when he or she was born, they were going to get just that.

"Have you had the test, by the way? You keep saying he."

She shook her head. "I'm not going to have it, but I just have a feeling in my gut it's a mini-James. But if it's not, that's fine, too. I'm going to get gender-neutral gear anyway. Even if the baby is born one gender, it doesn't mean they're going to stay that way forever, does it? I've been in teaching long enough to know that."

I smiled. "You are officially the most forward-thinking parent I've ever met. Promise me one thing, too. If it's a girl, please don't put a pink band on her head with a bow on it?"

Kerry let out a booming laugh. "If I ever do that, shoot me, okay?"

I threaded an arm through hers and we strolled down

the aisles, taking in the abundance of stuff on offer. "Maybe I should branch out of cakes and go into maternity and kids' stuff. Have you seen the price on this?" I was holding up a baby beanbag, price tag £69. I was sure you could get one down the market far cheaper.

"There's tons of money in kids. Have you only just realised?"

We walked down another aisle, Kerry fondling a lemon and yellow blanket, which we decided was sufficiently gender-neutral. We were both also taken with a cuddly lion.

"If you buy it, don't call it Lenny. Call it Lisa. Lisa The Lion is way better."

Kerry grinned, picking Lisa up. "I can't leave Lisa behind now, can I?" She paused, tucking Lisa under her arm. "You know who's been brilliant since the funeral?"

I shook my head, picking up a pair of lemon booties with bright-red pom-poms on the back. When I saw they cost £45, I dropped them like they were burning my hand.

"Maddie."

That made me turn my head. "Really?"

"Yes. She's been driving over to see me, ringing me to see if I need anything. I never thought of all the people in my life, the one who rallied would be Maddie."

"Life takes strange turns, as we know."

Kerry shook her head. "I'm still mad at James for keeping secrets about her, but I've learned you're not allowed to be mad at dead people. Once you die, you get some sort of saintly halo which means nobody can ever speak ill of you."

"Is that right?"

"It is." Kerry gulped and looked away.

Next to her head, a giant giraffe was lit up, with a sticker on its tummy that said 'press me'. Kerry reached out and did just that. The giraffe began to sing, telling Kerry it loved her. In moments, her body was shaking from laughter, not tears.

"I should remember to come in here when I'm feeling low. Although once the baby's born, that might make me cry a bit more." She shook her head. "How the fuck did my life end up like this? Widowed and pregnant at 34. I'm like one of those stories you read in 'That's Life' magazine."

"Your hair's much shinier than any of those women in that sad rag. Plus, you're only knocked up with your husband's child. Call that a scandal? They wouldn't."

Kerry put her arm around me and kissed my cheek. "I've missed you, let's see more of each other."

"Deal." I glanced sideways. "Although it's not for want of trying. Since the funeral, you've been booked more than the Rolling Stones."

"I know. Blame my family. I love them, but it's time to get back to normal life now. Well, as normal as things can ever be."

We turned the next corner, and came across a huge range of babygrows, all with those twee catchphrases on. Kerry stopped at one that said 'Mama ain't raisin' no fool', with an illustration of a baby raisin on it. She took it off the peg. "My first babygrow purchase. A monumental moment." She trailed off and I wondered if she was thinking of James. I was.

"Although it's not the first baby thing I have. Maddie bought me a really cool Ramones babygrow, which I can't wait to use." She glanced at me to gauge my reaction. "Have you seen her at all?"

I cleared my throat, feeling a blush rise to my cheeks. "Yep, I've seen her. More than I thought. Would you believe she's taking me to view a property tomorrow?"

Kerry's eyebrows were so raised, I thought they might fly off her head.

"And yes, I know, this is a turn of events."

"I'll say. You wanted to kill her at James's funeral."

I sighed. "I did. But murder at a funeral is frowned upon. I'm not really one to shirk societal norms. Plus, James's funeral reminded me that life's short. If she's back in our lives, I'd rather be civil to her. Especially as she's proving useful."

Kerry nodded. "And she seems genuinely sorry about the past." Kerry grabbed a basket and sat Lisa The Lion in it, along with the babygrow. "She was very keen to point that out to me when I met her for lunch last week. I think that was more for your benefit than mine, but whatever. I appreciated the sentiment."

"She said the same to me, but don't get carried away. Even though I can't help feeling things when I'm with her, I think it's mainly nostalgia. No matter how great Maddie seems now, I still remember how I felt when she left last time, and I'm not putting myself in that position again."

"I know." Kerry gave me a smile, but I wasn't quite sure what it said. Then she held up the babygrow in front of my face. "Yes or no on this?"

"You have my full blessing. And for Lisa."

"Good." She dropped the babygrow back in the basket, taking my hand and giving it a squeeze. "But you know, if things change with you and Maddie, you won't be losing face with your friends by giving it another go. Just in case you were wondering. We want you to be happy, and like you said, life is short."

"It's not happening. Why does everyone think that? My mum nearly had heart failure when I told her I'd seen Maddie. I make good decisions all the time in my life, I'm not suddenly just going to fold because Maddie has waltzed back into my life."

"Maybe it's because you two were more than just a couple. We all thought you were destined. You were good together."

"*Were* being the operative word." I sighed. "She changed that when she left, didn't she?" I shook my head, my emotions swirling around me again. Whenever Maddie was brought into the conversation, it happened every time. "Anyway, let's not tarnish Junior's first purchase. Shall we pay and go for lunch?"

Kerry nodded, then walked towards the till.

Chapter Fifteen

Maddie picked me up in her dirty white work van, which wasn't what I'd expected. There was me thinking property developing was a glamour job, but Maddie laughed when I said that.

"Far from it. I tried having a cool car for a while, but you soon realise if you spend half your life on building sites and the other half in the Wickes car park, it's a bit stupid to rock up in a car where you're worried about the paint work. You've already seen my Mini, but my brother's borrowing it at the moment. Sorry if this is a little downmarket for you."

I brushed the seat, shaking my head as I got in. "It's fine. What's a bit of dust between friends?"

I glanced over at Maddie, who gave me a grin that made my stomach flip-flop. It took me right back to the summer of our final year, lying in the park, my head on Maddie's taut stomach. Then, I'd have bet the house on us. Which just went to show what terrible judgement I had.

The intervening years flashed before my eyes. What the hell was I even doing in a car with this woman who'd ripped my heart out?

"Is that what we are? Friends?" My tone was acidic.

Maddie's sure grin turned slightly less so. "I hope we're that, at the very least."

She slammed the driver's door and started the engine. Her face went through a myriad of poses, before she arrived at the one she thought most appropriate for taking a drive with me, her ex-love.

She pulled out, careful not to glance my way, keeping her eyes on the road. There were so many questions I had wanted to ask since she strolled back into my life, but I didn't know where to start. My heart raced and my throat was dry as we hurtled towards the city centre at a rate I was sure was faster than the speed limit. Still, I wasn't going to point that out when I couldn't even clear my throat or wrap my tongue around the basics of what I wanted to say. Like, why the hell did you really leave? It must have been more than fear of commitment?

We drove through the centre, past the waterfront, and past Wapping Wharf. I tensed as I looked towards The Spanish Station. When I glanced left, Maddie's knuckles were white on the steering wheel, her gaze fixed straight ahead. I wasn't sure what had gone on in five minutes, but this wasn't what happened when you were just friends. I had enough of those relationships, I knew the drill. This tense static in the air, the type you could slice and toast, was very much relationship tension. Stuff gone unsaid tension. I found myself holding my breath.

Ten minutes later, we pulled up at the property in

Archer Street. I'd never been more pleased to end a journey. I'd gone to speak a few times, and so had Maddie, but neither of us had broken the deadlock. Despite that, when Maddie stood next to me outside the building, my body prickled with heat. I wondered if she noticed too, as she took a step away as the property agent arrived. The woman had peroxide blonde hair and black-rimmed glasses with tailored black trousers and a white lacy top. She looked more suited to a fashion house than an estate agent, but it made a refreshing change from men with too much hair gel and bad ties.

"Great to see you, I'm Nora."

We all shook hands, Nora's handshake firmer than I expected.

"It's so exciting that you're both looking at this. What sort of business are you hoping to install here? Was it something to do with cakes? Because if that's right, count me in. Everyone loves cake, don't they?"

From the look on both our faces, you'd think the answer to that question was no. Nora frowned and cocked her head. "Did I get that wrong?"

I broke first. "No, I run a cake school. But it's me and my business partner. Maddie's a…" I couldn't bring myself to fill in the blank. I cleared my throat. "She's just helping me look for the ideal property."

I put my head down and followed Nora through the door.

It was only when I was fully inside that I stopped and

my jaw went slack. This place was incredible. Huge, with a massive wall of glass at the front that meant the light streamed in. Our business was selling a certain lifestyle, and this was it. I could already feel myself softening to Maddie. She might have been my downfall in the past, but she was doing a good job of being my saviour in the present.

According to its history, this space had gone through many iterations in the past few years, from a storehouse to an office and most recently, a restaurant. Hence why Maddie had picked it out. It already had the right services and potential for our food-based business. I could see us doing classes and workshops here. Plus, there was enough space for a bigger kitchen. More storage, more business, and it was large enough for growth, too. I already knew what Gemma would say. More importantly, if it stuck close to the guide price, we could afford it.

I glanced over at Nora, then at Maddie, who was giving me a look I couldn't quite read.

"What do you think?" That was Nora. She was putting on her professional face, even though she was probably more than a little confused by the vibe coming from both of us. I knew I would be.

I gave her a nod. "It's perfect. A lot of work, but perfect. I just need to get my business partner to come over and have a look, so maybe we can arrange that for another time. Also my brother, who's a builder."

"A very handy brother to have!" Nora said.

"He has his moments." I paused. "What do you think?"

I was talking to Maddie now. She was the expert, after all, the one who found this place. Whatever reaction I might be having to her presence, I valued her opinion on this.

"I think it could be ideal. The location's great, too. But you've got to figure it out with Gemma. I know you're the one who needs convincing."

She was talking about the property, I was sure, but there was so much else that could have been read into it. I took a deep breath and walked into the kitchen, mentally checking what would need to be done. It was still so much, and such a massive proposition to move our operation lock, stock and barrel.

When I looked up, Maddie was leaning on the kitchen doorframe, staring at me. "It's a good option, Jus, and one you can afford. Think about it."

I nodded. "I will."

Maddie held my stare. "Give you a lift back?"

* * *

"How come your brother's got your car?" Going to the property had at least given us both something to concentrate on that wasn't the breakdown of our relationship all those years ago, and whether we could ever be friends again. Proper friends, not just superficial bullshit. We both settled into the van as Maddie adjusted her mirrors before starting the engine.

"He's going through a tough time. He lost his job because of Brexit, and it meant he lost his car, too. My

Mini only gets used at weekends or special occasions, so it's a long-term loan. I told him to treat it like his first-born, and he gave me a weird look." She grinned at me. "I've always been more into cars than him. I'd always wanted a Mini, and it was one of the first things I bought when I could afford it. If you'd asked me to give Harris my beloved car five years ago, I'd have looked at you weirdly." She shrugged. "But he needs it now, so it made sense." She drummed her fingers on the steering wheel. They were still long and slim, just like I remembered.

"Nice of you to do that, especially considering the up and down relationship you two had when we were together."

"Harris and I see each other a bit more, now. Shame we didn't do it earlier. Times change, people change."

I wondered if that was true. "You know, when I saw you pull up in your Mini, I noticed your car first before I knew it was you. I thought it was a little try-hard, a bit boy-racer."

Maddie pulled out onto the road. "That's very gender-specific of you." She kept her eyes focused on the traffic as she spoke. "Aren't women allowed to have racer-type cars, too?" I could hear the smile in her voice.

"They are, and you're right, it was very judgmental of me. Particularly when I'm not that different. As soon as I could afford it, I bought myself a green Golf, because that's what I always wanted when I was younger. So I get it." I rolled my neck as we approached Wapping Wharf. "Only I called my car Kermit. I bet you didn't name yours."

"Think again." A smile spread across Maddie's features. "What's it called?"

"Mavis."

My laugh pierced the van's air. "Perhaps we're not so different at all."

Maddie changed gear, then hung a left. "Maybe we're not," she replied, her voice low. "We always had a lot in common. It wasn't just chemistry and sexual attraction. Although that was off the chart." She glanced my way. "That much hasn't changed."

There was a fuzz in my head as I took in what she'd just said. But I couldn't deny it. It was in every step we took, every look we exchanged. It was hovering in the car now, as Maddie turned into the wharf car park. She waited until she cut the engine before she turned to me. "I was thinking maybe we could have a drink at The Spanish Station? For old times' sake. Plus, it's a gorgeous day, it'd be a shame to just go home and not sit in the sunshine, wouldn't it?"

Danger rippled deliciously through me, stopping to inspect every hair on my body. I ignored it. Maddie was right. It was a gorgeous day and we should make the most of it. Plus, despite all signs earlier, I was enjoying being with her. Hadn't Kerry told me the other day life was short? It was just a drink by the water, nothing more.

Although, if I was an undercover cop with a siren, I would have just taken it out and put it on my head.

Maddie's gaze slid down my body like honey as I walked around the car, and my insides wobbled.

I took a deep breath and told myself the score. It was just a drink with an old friend who was helping me out. I owed her that much for finding this property. It wasn't ours yet, but it might be. Maddie had done this for us, got us further than Gemma and I had done in a few months of looking.

But as we turned the corner and saw the bar, we both stopped in our tracks. Nothing had changed, and in that moment, it was like we'd time-travelled back to a more innocent time. Fairy lights were strung around the windows, currently off because the natural light was enough. Old barrels turned into tables sat outside with bar stools, and a chalkboard drilled into the bare brick wall told of the tapas on special tonight. The whitewashed walls were in need of a touch-up, and the striped awning had seen better days.

But all of that just added to the charm of the place. "You said earlier that things change. This place hasn't."

I glanced at Maddie, who turned to me. "Not one bit." She smiled. "Shall we sit?"

I nodded and we claimed a table, a tense smile settling on my face. Was this asking for trouble? After all, today of all days had been very up and down with emotion. However, we were here now. I was going to have to let it ride out and see where we landed.

A server dressed casually in jeans and a white T-shirt took our order, and we relaxed, taking in the waterside view. It was just as I recalled: boats bobbing, and the bars on either side of the harbour doing a vibrant trade. This end was always less packed, which is why we'd loved it then. The Spanish Station had given us some privacy, had been an incubator for our love. I took a breath as our drinks arrived: Sauvignon Blanc for me, craft beer for Maddie. We chinked glasses, and held each other's gaze.

I was glad I had my sunglasses on, as I feared my eyes would have given too much away. I wanted to turn the conversation onto safer topics than the past, but Maddie got there first.

"Did you know that Ally and Gemma are out on a date tonight, without Dean?"

I shook my head. They were? "I didn't. She's not said much about it, which isn't like Gemma. I'm not sure what it means."

"Probably that she likes her? I know Ally is very into her, because she keeps pumping me for info. But as I keep telling her, my knowledge of Gemma is very old, just like you really. I'd like to bring it up to speed, though. I hope I'll get the chance." She licked her lips as her gaze held me.

"I could say the same." My throat was dry as I spoke, so I took a gulp of my wine. "You told me a bit about your brother, but that was it. How's your mum?" I was curious to know. Maddie's mum had always been so supportive of her and everything she did, and if meeting Maddie again meant I could see Diane, too, that was another plus point. Diane was a liberal through and through, and had coped with her husband drinking too much for years with good grace, before eventually throwing him out when she discovered a string of affairs. Her brother Amos had moved in after that, and the pair had proved a real double act.

Maddie shifted on her stool, clutching her bottle of beer so tight, her knuckles went white. She wouldn't meet my gaze, before expelling a long breath.

This wasn't good news, was it?

"She died two years ago. Lung cancer. Even though she never smoked a cigarette in her entire life." She didn't take her eyes off the water ahead. Her jaw tightened, her breathing hitched.

My heart cracked into thousand tiny pieces, like a delicate Christmas bauble that's fallen from the tree. I reached out and put a hand on her thigh.

Maddie's muscles flinched beneath my fingertips, then relaxed, her gaze whipping around to me, before turning away again. She put a hand to her brow and ground her teeth together.

"I'm so sorry about your mum. I always loved her. I was only thinking about her the other day." Whatever was between us, I wouldn't wish losing a parent onto anyone.

"She loved you, too." Maddie glanced my way and gave me the saddest smile. "She was the best. It's been a hard couple of years." She was trying to control her breathing, but I could see she was struggling. "When she died, I used to come here. The first time I had since we broke up. It was comforting, somehow, I could sort of feel you, us. Mum really did love you, too."

"Was Amos still living with her?"

She took a swig of her beer before she replied. "He was, and he's been muddling on. But he's not the same, none of us are. I've been staying with him for about half the week since I've been back, making sure he's okay. It's been good spending time with him, and something I should have done with Mum. Something I'll always regret. I put work ahead of her, didn't realise how sick she was."

She exhaled. "And now Amos is ill, too. He was the main reason I wanted to move back this way because his health's failing. He's terminal, got bone cancer. Everybody's getting older or dying."

I clenched my calf muscles as I processed what Maddie had said. I still couldn't believe Diane was dead. "Fuck, I'm so sorry. It sounds like a dreadful couple of years." I paused. "So coming to James's funeral must have been tough for you."

She nodded ever so slowly. "You could say that. It was the first funeral I'd been to since Mum died. It was tougher for Kerry, though." Her shoulders sagged. "It was so lovely meeting with James again, and I was planning to say hi to everyone eventually. But then he got sick and that took over. Sometimes, life spirals away from you, doesn't it?"

"It does. Seems like a lot of things have changed since we were together. Not just us, but our whole lives, too."

She nodded, before turning back to me. "But anyway, let's not get all melancholy, not here. We're both still very much alive."

"True," I said. "But you must miss your mum."

She closed her eyes for a brief moment. "Like you wouldn't believe. Not having her here is like a raw ache inside, gnawing away. Like knowing whatever you eat, you're never going to be full. We didn't live together or see each other all the time, but just knowing she was there was enough. There are so many things I want to tell her, so many things I wished I'd asked. But it's too late." She opened her eyes fully and turned to me, putting a hand on my wrist. "Don't take your mum for granted, promise me?"

I shook my head. "I won't."

She ran the pad of her thumb over my wrist, and it felt so intimate.

I shivered, and when our gazes snagged, we both stilled. The conversation hadn't gone where I'd expected, and neither had my emotions.

"It's one of the reasons I've been going around to Kerry's to offer support. Because I understand what she's going through. I know it's different — losing a partner as opposed to a parent — but grief is grief. I've worked through it, and I'm still going. If I can help her, I want to. Grief is just love with nowhere to go."

That took my breath away. "Oh, Maddie." Sadness reached in and grabbed me. I shook my head, running a hand up and down her arm. If we were surprised at the touching at first, we were clearly getting used to it fast.

A few beats went by before I spoke again.

"You know, when we first met again, I wanted to kill you."

Maddie let out a snort of laughter. "That's not what I expected you to say."

"And you're not what I expected you to be. You're very different to the uncaring monster I'd built up in my mind. You're very far from that, in fact."

She smiled. "That's a good thing, right?"

"It is, but it's confusing."

She sighed. "I know we've got a lot to talk about, I know things are unfinished. I'd like to explain everything to you. I didn't want to do it fully before because you were too angry, and I don't blame you. But now…" She shrugged. "Maybe we could do it soon. Go out and I could talk about everything fully. Fill in the missing pieces of the puzzle."

I nodded. "Maybe we could." I held her stare. Saying that felt scary, but the only thing I could say. We needed to talk, to get everything out in the open.

"I know you don't trust me, but I'm going to try to change that."

I put a hand on her cheek and left it there. I was still winded by her news. "I'm so sorry about your mum. But she'd be proud of you for what you're doing for Amos."

Maddie leaned in to my palm. "I hope so."

Chapter Sixteen

The next day, I was still winded by Maddie's news. It'd been on my mind all the previous evening, and I'd half expected tears. They hadn't come. I couldn't quite believe Maddie's mum was dead, and Amos was dying.

Overnight, my view of her had changed. I still didn't know the whole story of why she'd left, but she was going to tell me. After that, I knew I might have a decision to make. But until then, I was going to avoid thinking about it too much. And what was the best way to avoid thinking about your own matters of the heart? Why, to focus on somebody else's, of course.

I drove Gemma over to the potential property the following evening after classes finished. "A little bird told me you had a date last night."

Gemma shook her head, but she wriggled in her seat. Busted.

"What?" I threw her a grin. "Since when did we get coy about what was happening in our dating lives? You've always told me before, but it seems when it comes to Ally, you're being exactly that. You've been on two whole dates now, and you've been uncharacteristically silent. Which either means she's a terrible kisser — but then, you went on a second date, so I'm counting that one out. The only other option left is that she's stunned you into silence with her witty repartee and her amazing sex. I'm going for option two."

"I don't have to tell you everything that happens in my life." Gemma stared intently at her phone, studiously ignoring me.

I pulled up at some lights and glanced over, to see she'd opened the Daily Mail website. "You shouldn't be looking at that. It fuels their advertising and so their negative impact on the world." It wasn't the first time I'd pointed this out.

"Okay, Saint Justine. I'll try not to look ever again," Gemma replied, as she always did.

I nudged her with my elbow. "So tell me. Why so quiet?" The lights went green and I pulled away.

Gemma gave me a slow shrug, and then wriggled again. The amount of wriggling was not lost on me. "I dunno. It's just, she's… different. I don't want to speak about anything too soon and jinx it, that's all. But she's gorgeous. Also, intelligent, hot, solvent. And she's got the cool northern accent going on. You know how I love an accent."

"I do." Gemma had once gone out with a Geordie and when they'd split up, she'd saved a voicemail the woman had left her for over a year.

"Yeah, well... She's kinda the full package, which is a bit scary. But we're not putting any labels on it yet, it's too soon. At the moment, it's just an arrangement."

I raised an eyebrow. "An arrangement? It sounds like you're in a bad TV movie. Are you exclusive?"

Gemma sighed. "I think so. At least, I am." Another sigh. "I do really like her, but I'm keeping this on the downlow for now. Plus, you're in touch with Maddie, so that makes it even weirder. I mean, I've never started dating someone who's best friends with someone you know so well. And anyway, we're not dating, we're seeing each other."

I frowned. "And the difference is?"

Gemma huffed. "Shuddup."

"I don't even know Maddie that well anymore."

Gemma gave me a look. "You kinda do. I mean, yes, I know you've only just reconnected, but you don't forget everything that went before, do you? You haven't seen each other for years, but you know the in-depth stuff about each other. Once you've done that with someone, it's only a small step to get back there again. All of which means that telling you anything about Ally is odd. I don't want things to get back to Maddie."

I stared at her, not quite following her logic. "You're giving Maddie and I way too much credit. You should have seen us yesterday in the car on the way over to Archer Street. The past was pressing down on us so hard, it was unbelievable. We still haven't really talked, and until we do, we can't move forward. So we're not quite in the place you imagine. We're not texting, meeting up for drinks, any of that. All Maddie and I are doing at the moment is dancing around each other."

"Didn't you go for a drink yesterday after you saw the place?"

I nodded. "We did, but that was the first time I felt a little... normal around her. And it was only for an hour." I paused, pulling into Archer Street and thinking back to how awkward yesterday had been here. "But it was good to get that hour, I have to admit."

"If it helps, Ally has nothing but good things to say about her." Gemma paused. "Did you know one of the reasons Maddie came back was to look after her sick uncle?"

I nodded, doom slipping through me as I remembered Diane was dead. If it had the power to floor me, I couldn't imagine what it did to Maddie. Every time something happened, did she reach for her phone to call her mum, and then stop? "She's had a rough couple of years, what with her mum dying, too."

"From everything Ally tells me, she hasn't done much for herself over the past few years. She's been there for her mum, her uncle and brother. So I don't think you need to be so wary."

I sighed. "Until we talk, nothing's changed. And even then, I'm not sure anything can." I rolled my neck from side to side. "Anyway, nice try on moving the chat away from Ally."

Gemma grinned at me. "You're not getting anything

out of me yet. Let's just say, I'm happy where things are. She's a breath of fresh air."

"Good." I cut the engine, pulling on the handbrake outside the Archer St site. "This is it."

Gemma whistled as she got out of Kermit, putting a hand up to her brow to shield it from the sun. She walked up and down the front of the building, peering inside, her nose against the glass. I hadn't been able to get the agent to meet us tonight, so Gemma was going to have to rely on my running commentary and imagine what it felt like inside. She could still get a good idea of the space from the front, though. Plus, as she'd said on the drive over, why wouldn't you spend all this money on something you'd never seen the inside of? It made perfect sense.

"This looks ideal." She pulled her face away, wiping the tip of her nose as she did. "And if you and Maddie loved it inside, that's good enough for me." She stared at me. "You did love it, right?"

I nodded. "As much as I can love a project, yes. But Maddie thought it was great, and she had a lot of ideas of what we could do." I pointed through the window. "Two workshops in the main space, big kitchen at the back and an office each. Or whatever we wanted." I stood back. "But it's big enough, the location's great and we can afford it."

Gemma gave me a decisive nod. "That's what I was thinking." She spun around. "I think this could be Cake Heaven, phase two."

With Kerry's money as our deposit, we had the mortgage

secured in principle from the bank. Now the only thing standing in our way was a final decision to go for it. Then, of course, we had to win the property auction. But seeing Gemma's reaction made up my mind 99 per cent.

"I think you might be right." I sucked in a lungful of air through my teeth, my shoulders hunching as my muscles tightened. "Is this the right move?"

Gemma walked over to me and put her hand on my shoulder. "I don't know. But there's only one way to find out." She paused. "Are you telling me you're almost convinced?"

I visualised our current location, all the hours we'd put in getting it perfect. Dean had made the space exactly what we wanted with worktops, offices and sockets where we needed them. He could do it again, I knew. So what was I scared of?

Our demand was already outstripping what we could do, so a move was the perfect solution. I peered through the glass again, before swivelling back to Gemma. "What if nobody likes it here, though? What if we can't sell the classes?" Fear spilled out of me like a river.

Gemma squeezed me again. "You had the same fear when we stopped doing the classes at our flats and fitted out our current space. But it worked out, didn't it? And you know what they say: everything you really want is just outside your comfort zone. If you're scared, that's a good thing. And you're not alone, we're in this together. I've got faith in our marketing skills — well, mine at least." She gave me a grin. "And I'll let you into a secret:

I'm scared, too, but I'm also excited. They're basically the same emotion."

Excitement mixed with fear was what I felt with Maddie, who was definitely outside my comfort zone. But was she what I wanted? I still wasn't sure. But Gemma wasn't talking about Maddie. She was talking about what we could do to take our business to the next level.

Everything in life was a gamble. Nothing was set in stone. Our business gamble had paid off before, and there was no reason to think it wouldn't again. Cake Heaven had been great so far: but could it be even greater? Like Gemma said, there was only one way to find out. I turned to her, giving what I hoped was a confident smile. "Let's do it. Let's go to the auction next week and bid. We'll set a limit on the bidding, but I think we should try."

Gemma swept me up in her arms, squeezing me tight. "I say this is a monumental decision for Cake Heaven and one you won't regret." She squeezed one more time, before holding me at arm's length. "You sure about this? Positive you want to do it?"

I nodded. "As positive as I can be."

"Good enough for me."

Chapter Seventeen

My hand was sweaty around the white plastic paddle, inscribed with the number 435. Why was it everybody else looked far more at ease than I did? Beside me, Gemma was gripping my knee, checking the catalogue for our lot: we were still a few numbers off. We were lucky we were early in the bidding. If we'd have been lot 134 instead of lot 16, it would have been a very long day. On the other side of me, Maddie gave me encouraging smiles, in between chatting to Dean.

Dean was beyond excited because it had been announced at the beginning of the auction that 'Homes Under The Hammer' were here and filming. They told the auction crowd ahead of time in case there were people who didn't want to be on camera — they only filmed one side of the room. The look Dean had given me when they'd announced they were filming was priceless.

"Fucking hell, that is my absolute dream. So many of my mates have been on it, and I've always wanted to. Can you imagine someone not wanting to?" Dean clearly couldn't. He'd grasped my arm. "If you get on, promise me I can come with you and be your builder friend."

Dean could be weird, had I mentioned that? "No you can't. You can come along and be my builder brother, because that's what you are."

He'd looked like I'd given him my last Rolo, and then pulled me into a bear hug. I hoped we got on, otherwise Dean would be crushed. But first, I had the small matter of bidding on the property, not spontaneously combusting, and somehow managing to win it. Piece of cake.

Dean leaned over Maddie and tapped my arm. "You want a coffee?"

I shook my head, my brow creased. I checked the catalogue: two lots away. I couldn't multitask right now, what was he thinking? It was enough to raise a paddle in the air and spend more than I ever had done in my life. As every lot was announced, Gemma and I had been concentrated on staying very still, lest we buy a house by accident.

I'd watched my share of 'Homes Under The Hammer', and this space perfectly reflected what I'd seen there. A stuffy hotel function room filled with rows of padded chairs, cheap gold paint flaking off the legs. A jittery crowd waiting for their lot to come up. I'd only ever been in betting shops on Grand National day, but the auction house had an air of that about it. All the oxygen had been sucked from the air, and the experienced bidders stood at the back so they could see all the action. Maddie had insisted we sit near the back for that reason. "That way, we can see the enemy when your lot comes up." We were going to war.

Dean got back to his seat just in time, giving me a thumbs up as our lot was announced. Gemma was wriggling in her seat beside me, the way she did whenever I mentioned Ally. I sat up, holding my breath. We'd decided beforehand that I was the more level-headed of the two of us, the one most likely to stick to our plans. Therefore, I had the bidding paddle. Now, I really wished it was Gemma. I bit down too hard in my mouth and tasted blood. I winced. Not a good start.

Beside me, Maddie grabbed my free hand and squeezed. I shook a little. She put her lips beside my ear. "You've got this," she whispered, dropping my hand and giving me a wink.

I didn't have time to process how that made me feel as the bidding got under way. All of sudden, my brain took over and I was engaged, sitting out the first few bids as Maddie had instructed, taking in the competition before entering the race. I really hoped we didn't have a bidder who pushed the price up too much, but I'd know soon enough.

At Maddie's prompt, I raised my paddle to enter the race, my hand clammy around it. We were off; as was my heartbeat. The auctioneer's patter was lyrical, but all I heard was the bid level, slowly creeping up. I kept raising my paddle, but so did a man a few rows ahead. I took a deep breath. It was between the two of us.

In what seemed like a breathless wheeze of time, we

were reaching the guide price. I clutched the paddle that little bit tighter. "This is getting a bit squeaky bum," I hissed. Jesus, if I'd have known it was going to be this stressful, I'd have given the paddle to Maddie.

Beside me, Gemma's knees were going up and down at a rate of knots, and my heart was racing so fast, it might need an emergency pit stop. We were now over the guide price by 20 grand, but the bid was with us. Our top level was 50 grand over.

Please stop, please stop. I craned my neck to try to give the balding rival bidder a death stare, but he wasn't looking at me. His eyes were firmly planted to the front.

"What if he doesn't stop bidding?" I asked Maddie.

She pulled her lips into a straight line and shook her head. "Just concentrate on what you're doing, don't worry about anyone else." She sounded like my mum when I was stressing about my exams.

I huffed, but did as I was told. Thirty grand over now. Shit, were we about to be outbid? From not wanting the space, I'd now come full circle, where it was fully mine. If somebody else snatched it from my grasp, I'd be distraught.

Then suddenly, the other bidder stopped. My heart thundered in my ears.

He dropped his paddle and shook his head.

I sat up straighter like a meerkat, facing the auctioneer full on. He was pointing at me with one hand, a mallet raised in the other.

"With you madam," he told me. "Anybody else, last

bids? Anyone got a few more grand burning a hole in their pocket?"

I wanted to clock him over the head with his own mallet. Stop encouraging them! *Breathe, breathe.* How did Maddie do this all the time? I feared I might die of heart failure.

"Going once, going twice…" Why did the silence seem to stretch on for days? "Sold!" The sound of wood on wood signalled the property was ours, and then I was engulfed in a flurry of hugs from all sides.

"We did it!" That was Gemma's voice, emerging from the impromptu pile-on. "Cake Heaven is go!"

She was right. We'd done it. And for as long as I lived, I hoped I never had to go to an auction again. My nerves were shredded. I untangled myself and we all filed out of the auction, grins wide, adrenaline at peak.

It wasn't until I got out of the main room and into the corridor that I flung my arms in the air like I was in the final scenes of a redemption movie. "Aaaaah!" I yelped. "We only went and fucking did it! We bought a new premises." I frowned. "We have to come up with a new word. Premises is rubbish."

Dean put an arm around me and ruffled my hair. I hated him. He knew that annoyed me.

"Do that again and you're not coming on 'Homes Under The Hammer'."

His face fell. "You wouldn't." But I could tell by the quiver in his voice he wasn't sure.

I couldn't stop my smile. "Don't test me." I blew out a

long breath and balled my fists, before clearing my throat and standing up straight. I had a lot of pent-up energy I needed to expel. "Right, let's go sort the paperwork out, and then we're going for a glass of wine. After that, I deserve it."

* * *

We got a seat in the Watchmaker's Arms over the road from the auction house. I was surprised Dean was still in one piece and hadn't combusted over the table. After Gemma and I had signed the documents and dealt with the admin, the team from 'Homes Under The Hammer' had approached us and asked about our time scales, and whether they could follow our journey. So now it was official: we were going to be TV stars.

"A toast." Dean held up his glass. "To Maddie. For coming back into my sister's life, suggesting going to an auction, giving me work and ultimately making my 'Homes Under The Hammer' dreams come true. You're an absolute legend in my eyes, even though Justine might think otherwise."

Gemma made a sound like a donkey. I sat, mouth open, staring first at Dean, then at Maddie. Had he really said that? Like he was 12 and didn't understand the complexity of human relationships at all? Perhaps he didn't. Perhaps that's why he was single. It would explain a great deal.

"Thanks, Dean." I was pleased to see Maddie didn't quite know how to take that, either. "Glad your dreams are coming true. Let's hope it follows through with everyone here, shall we?" When she spoke, she didn't take her eyes from me, before holding up her glass again, and waiting until we all followed suit. "To the continued success of Cake Heaven. And to all our dreams coming true, whatever they may be."

I gulped as she spoke. I was sure there were lines to read between, but I was leaving them well alone.

Chapter Eighteen

Kerry turned up at Rob's bakery for lunch looking like Kerry, but also seven months pregnant. I'd last seen her three weeks ago, and in that time, she'd swelled up and looked like she had a bowling ball under her jumper. I was about to tell her exactly that when Kerry held up a hand, her fair curls newly cut. She didn't look like a pregnant widow. She looked stunning.

"If you tell me I've swollen up and look like I'm about to drop any minute, I might punch you. Fair warning."

I kept my mouth tight shut. "The thought never even crossed my mind."

"Good." Kerry pulled out a chair and sat down, groaning as she did. "I hope Rob's got that lovely quiche he makes today, otherwise there might be hell to pay. My hormones are all over the shop. Anything sets me off, not just stuff to do with James. In fact, if anything, I prefer it when it's down to James. At least my husband dying is a valid thing to cry about. But crying about them not having any oat milk in the Co-Op? That was a bit much. I think the assistant thought I was barking mad."

I laughed. "Or perhaps really in love with oat milk."

Kerry rubbed her stomach, staring at it for a moment, before looking up. She'd zoned out for a moment, but was now back in the room. "Good to see you. You're looking…" She paused and looked me up and down, as if assessing me for sale. "You're looking like someone who's about to do big things. Am I right?"

I gave her a grin. "Gemma said she called you."

Kerry nodded. "Congratulations. Glad to see my money being spent so quickly. How are you feeling?"

"Scared shitless, but also pretty happy. This feels like a monumental shift. And can I say again, we couldn't have done this without you? Without your investment, none of this would be possible."

Kerry waved a hand. "I'm a business woman, and investing in you two was a no-brainer. I know I'll get my money back. I believe in you, so be happy."

I smiled at her. "I'm glad you do, because sometimes, I'm not sure I believe in myself." I paused. "I mean, when it comes to the business, I totally do. But for everything else? It's not quite as straight forward."

"I assume this is to do with Maddie?"

I nodded. "Have you seen her lately?"

Kerry adjusted her posture before she replied. "Yup. She came over the other week and brought me dinner."

Now I felt bad. "Did she?"

"Stopped and picked it up on the way around. She pulled up in her van, which made me laugh. Somehow, I've always seen Maddie as a high-powered exec, but the reality is very different. Plus, she turned up wearing a toolbelt. I told her if she was going for the ultimate lesbian look, she was scoring high, but I wasn't her ideal audience. She blushed. It was kinda cute."

Every word in Kerry's sentence crawled down my body, and settled somewhere around my navel, which was now softly pulsing. I really hoped I wasn't blushing, too. The thought of Maddie in a toolbelt sent shockwaves through my system. The thought of Maddie in a toolbelt with nothing else on at all.

Hang on, I was thinking thoughts of Maddie naked when I was with my straight, widowed, pregnant friend? I was truly going to hell.

"Have you seen her in a toolbelt? I know having her back in your life must be all kinds of confusing, but at least if you saw that, it'd remind you *why*. Because she's bloody gorgeous. I always thought she looked quite feminine when she was younger, but I think this job of hers means she gets to unleash her more butch side."

Kerry snorted. "Mind you, I think living without a man means you can unleash your butch side whether you like it or not. I never realised how gender-based James and I were in what we did around the house, but we were. I don't think I've cut the grass since we moved in, and I've certainly never changed a fuse or a light bulb, or done any of those supposedly 'boy' jobs. Which is shit for a modern woman like me, isn't it? I mean, I used to do them, but as the years have gone on, something changed."

I laughed. "So that's a positive about James dying? You remembered how to change a light bulb?"

"Something like that." She sighed. "I fucking miss him, though. I miss him here." She covered her heart with her fist. "Sometimes I lie in bed in the morning, and I try to conjure up his voice or the sound of his footsteps on the stairs. Some days I can, and some days I can't, and that really freaks me out. I'm glad I've got videos of him on my phone for when I'm ready to hear his voice, but I think it might crush me."

I leaned over and covered her hand in mine. "You're doing amazingly well, but you're not going to get over this in a flash. This is something that's going to take a long time, so you need to accept that."

"I have." She sighed. "But sometimes, I want to rewind and have one last week with him. Just to tell him all my thoughts, all my fears, all my dreams. To make sure he knew how much I loved him." She closed her eyes. When she reopened them, they were glistening. "Do you think he knew how much I loved him? Because sometimes, I wonder. Did I tell him enough? Those final weeks are a blur."

My heart broke for her. I couldn't imagine what it had been like for Kerry — or what it was like for her now. I was on my feet and putting my arms around her before I had a chance to think, kissing her cheek, pulling her close. When I pulled away, Kerry shook her head and reached into her bag to pull out a pack of tissues. She blew her nose to get rid of her excess snot. I wiped her tears from my cheek as I sat down, swallowing down all my emotion.

I still hadn't shed a tear for James. Had Kerry noticed I had a heart of stone? If she had, she'd said nothing. I still felt like a total shit. Why couldn't I cry? What emotional valve had Maddie removed when she'd left me all those years ago and made me cry until there were no more tears? Perhaps I needed to Google it. Google normally knew the answers.

Or perhaps Maddie knew the answers. Perhaps I really did need to talk to her properly, to get over whatever angst was still in me, as evidenced in the car the other day. Maybe if I talked to Maddie properly, it would unlock something. Perhaps. For now, Maddie wasn't my prime worry. Kerry was. Kerry, and everything she needed. I should be taking dinners over to Kerry more often. Especially if Maddie was doing it.

"Do you still love Maddie?"

Wow, that question came out of the blue. "No, of course I don't. And even if I did, it's irrelevant, I told you that."

She stared at me for a long moment before replying. "Take a look at me, Justine. A long, hard look. And when you're finished, remember what I was crying about. In my heart, I think James knew I loved him, but I don't think he *truly* knew how much. Because nobody ever can, can they?

"The only person who knows how much love is inside

them is you. Because it's your love. I know I keep saying life is short, but it is. And if you've got *any* love inside you for Maddie — no matter what size it is — you owe it to yourself to talk to her, see what she has to say. She told me you've been avoiding her since the auction."

I hunched over. "I'm still not sure of myself around her, that's all."

"You should be. She told me some things the other night that explained why she did what she did. It wasn't the smartest decision she's ever made, but at least it explains it. And I know she still has love for you."

"She told you why she left?" That made me sit up. It was also a punch to the gut.

Kerry nodded. "She's been coming over to get me to talk about my grief. We've talked about her mum, too, as well as a bit about her last decade."

"Why hasn't she told me?"

"She's scared. Plus, she's not sure you'll even listen to her. But I think you should. The person you fell in love with is still there, and she wants you back in her life."

"She told you that?" My heart thundered in my chest.

"She didn't have to, it was written all over her face. So what I'm saying is this." She paused. "I'd give everything I own — *all of it* — to have one more chance with James. Life is just a string of relationships with people you love. Friends and family truly are all that matters.

"So if Maddie is one of those important people for you, at least listen to what she's got to say. You've been given another chance to connect, and who knows where it might lead? Make my dreams come true and do it for me, even if not for you. And, if in the end, you don't like what you hear, you can blame me. But I've spent time with Maddie, and I think there's something there for you. But only you know how much love you still have for her."

I was pondering my response when Rob walked over, flashing us both a smile. "Ladies. What would you like?"

That was the burning question, wasn't it?

Chapter Nineteen

A week later, after the schools went back and summer was having its final September splurge, we signed the papers and picked up the keys. Stepping into the space as owners made it all the more real, so much so that Gemma and I laughed when it happened. But then we'd hugged. This truly was a momentous occasion.

Maddie drove over to pick me up later that day.

I'd decided to let her in.

She was in her dusty van again, even though I'd tried to tell her I would drive. She'd insisted she was passing my way anyhow, and that we could head back to Bath for a picnic in the early evening sunshine. If I didn't know better, I'd swear it was a date. Was it a date? I honestly didn't know.

I saw her van pass our front window and was immediately warmed. I'm not sure when Maddie and I had turned the corner on our new relationship — whatever that was — but it seemed we were now friends, no longer stuck in that odd place where neither of us was quite sure what we were. Somewhere, between viewing our new empire (what we'd decided to call it) and buying it, we'd thawed to a certain point. We still had to air all the things we'd never said. I wasn't looking forward to that, because I knew it could make or break what we had. And as Gemma had told me earlier, friends or not, we needed to keep Maddie on-side throughout this process.

She strolled up to the door, looking elegantly cool in her white jeans, white Converse and blue T-shirt. Her V-neck exposed the skin on her chest nicely, and I tried not to stare. Her blonde hair licked her face like sunshine. Maddie knocked on the door, before sticking her tongue out at me.

I laughed as I unlocked it. "Sticking your tongue out? Really? Very mature."

"I never claimed to be mature."

She never claimed to be sexy, either, but that was the only word on the tip of my tongue as I took in her tall physique and her toned, tanned arms. I also loved the lines of her body, flowing and elegant. I shook myself and walked over to one of our tall fridges, getting out the food I'd bought earlier. "I hope you're hungry, because I went mad on the three-for-two picnic range in M&S." My mum would kill me for paying full price.

When I looked up, Maddie's gaze was focused; on what, I couldn't determine. My arse? My tits? Me? Or perhaps it was the spinach-and-pea feta parcels in my hand she found alluring. I cleared my throat and decided to keep things business-like. Above board. It's when you went overboard that things got messy.

"Who doesn't love M&S food? Plus, I'm starving."

Maddie rolled her gaze down my body, then back up, stopping on my face. "I hope there's something sweet to finish off with, too."

I ground my teeth together. *Focus!* Focus back on the food, back on the moment, back on the picnic. "There's cake, of course." That's what she'd been talking about, right? "Where are we going to eat? Bath?" Words were good to fill the air. Better than feelings.

Much better than feelings.

"I was thinking we could drive back to the Royal Crescent flat and picnic in the park. There's a little festival going on tonight, so it'll be lovely. I've even got a picnic blanket in my van. And it's brand-new, so not dusty at all."

"Are you trying to impress me?"

"I might be." With that she gave me her famous grin and I bit the inside of my cheek.

Then a thought occurred to me: I needed to reply to an email about the new empire. I'd been meaning to do it all day, and plain forgot. I frowned. "You mind if I send off a quick email about the new place? Otherwise, it'll be on my mind all night. I'll be five minutes."

Maddie shook her head. "Be my guest. I know what it's like running your own business, remember?"

She did, didn't she? That was another tick in the Maddie box. Was I keeping score? Apparently.

"Plus, I want your full attention later."

Had her voice got lower, too? It seemed that way. I exhaled. "I'll be quick."

Fifteen minutes later, I packed up the food into a cooler, put in some cake and gave it to Maddie. Our hands touched as I did so, and it was like a pressure valve being released under my ribs. I caught my breath. We both stared. All I could hear was the boom of my heart in my ears. I wasn't going to shake, that would be ridiculous.

I cleared my throat before I spoke. "I'll switch everything off and lock up. You go out to the van."

She nodded, poking her tongue into the side of her mouth, before doing what she was told.

I'd turned all the lights off and was by the door when Maddie appeared again, still with the picnic in her hand. She was wearing a frown.

"Everything okay?" I already knew it wasn't. I glanced down the road. Her van wasn't there.

She was shaking her head. "Can you believe my van's been stolen? I only got here like 20 minutes ago." She came inside and put the food down, her body taut. "How could it be stolen when we were right here?" She blew out a long breath, walking up and down the studio before turning to me. "This is really not what I need at the moment. That van's got all my stuff in it." She paused, a hand tangling in her hair. "Do I call 999? Is it an emergency?"

I held up a hand. "I don't think so, unfortunately." A dawning realisation sank through me. "Also, I don't necessarily think it's been stolen. The council are over-zealous when it comes to towing. Gemma's car's been done a few times, as has Rob's."

"In such a short space of time?"

"It only takes five minutes." I sighed. "Sorry, this is my fault for holding us up." I walked back towards my office. "Shall I get the number of the car pound first and see if it's been towed? Once we establish that, then we can report it stolen if it has been."

Maddie was nodding. "Yes please. At least if it's been towed, I can get it back." She shook her head. "So much for our romantic picnic."

I stopped, a warmth flooding through me. I turned to Maddie. "It was going to be romantic?"

She blushed, looking a little startled. "All picnics a bit romantic, aren't they?"

I didn't push her.

We got the number of the car pound, and after being put on hold for ten minutes, Maddie was told that yes, her van had been towed. Her relief was palpable. She signalled she needed a pen and paper, and when I gave it to her she scribbled something down, before hanging up.

"Little fuckers must be waiting to pounce." She threw her head back. "But at least it's not stolen." Another long sigh.

"It's a triumph, of sorts." I gave her a peppy smile. "So what now? Should I drive and you can pick the van up tomorrow?"

She furrowed her brow, shaking her head. "The thing is, I need the van early tomorrow. The guy on the phone said I could get it from this address in a couple of hours."

She held up the piece of paper. "Can you drive me there so we can get it? Sorry to bugger up our evening."

I shook my head. "No problem. We can pick up your van, then carry on with our evening a little later than planned."

"This wasn't in the brief, was it?"

I shrugged. "Life doesn't always go to plan, does it?"

Chapter Twenty

We drove over to Maddie's family home, which was all sorts of weird for me. Probably for Maddie, too, but she wasn't going to show it. Either that, or she had too much on her mind to entertain such thoughts. As we weaved through the streets, narrow and cluttered with cars, memories flooded my mind. Surprisingly, I found they only made me smile.

When we were at university, we'd come back here in the summer months. We'd both stayed at her mum's house and my parents' house, as well as house-sitting for friends when they were on holiday. Maddie and Diane had been so close, and a wave of something washed through me. The unfairness of life, perhaps? Of people dying too soon, before you got to say what you wanted to.

The house was a mid-terrace, three-storey affair, with an extension on the back with an amazing skylight. When I first visited more than a decade ago, it was the first house that truly took my breath away because of that. It was still the skylight and the kitchen I wanted to emulate when I bought my first home. Not having a kitchen skylight would be a deal-breaker.

I also recalled going to a party around here with Gemma a few years ago, and slowing down as I passed number 42. I'd wondered then about knocking on the door and saying hello to Diane, but had decided it might be a little weird. I wished I'd done it now, just to see her face one more time. Diane had been a one-off, so warm and welcoming to whoever arrived at her door. Some people touch you in life, and Diane had been one of those.

Her daughter was definitely another.

Maddie had her seatbelt off before I'd even cut the engine. "I need to nip in and get my documents, otherwise they're not going to give me the van. The fuckers." She turned to me. I could see there was a lot going on, and she wasn't quite sure how to say it. "You want to come in?" Her words dripped with hesitancy.

"Only if you want me to."

She frowned. "It might be a little weird, seeing as I remember bringing you back here before, and..." She glanced up at the bedroom window.

I knew what she was thinking, because I was thinking it too. It wasn't something easily forgotten.

"But then again, it might be even weirder leaving you in the car." She put a hand on the car door, then turned back. "Just so you know, Amos isn't in a good way. He's stage four cancer and it's in his bones. He can get around, but he's slow and in pain. So try not to react when you see him."

I nodded. "Got it. Smile at Amos. Don't think about you fucking me in the bedroom." I hadn't meant to say it, it just slipped out.

A semi-smile pierced Maddie's face. "Something like that." She turned to look at me fully.

The moment hung in the air for a beat.

Then two.

And then she opened the car door and got out.

I gripped the steering wheel, trying for the umpteenth time to make sense of where we were and what we were doing, but failing miserably. Only, I wasn't all that miserable. It had crossed my mind briefly before, but being with Maddie made me… happy? Content? In the moment?

Maddie stuck her head back in. "Are you coming?"

It was something I could ponder later. I unclipped my seatbelt and followed her into the house.

The kitchen was just as I remembered it. Warm evening rays spilled in, laying the loved wooden table with sunshine. Mismatched chairs were neatly tucked underneath, and two candles stood in the middle. The walls were bright white, reflecting the light around the room, giving a sense of space. This is what I wanted in my life, and I'd forgotten. I made a mental note to remember when I got home.

"This hasn't changed a bit." I walked over to the heart of the kitchen, the thick wooden worktops smooth under my fingertips. "I remember your mum cooking up all her fabulous dishes right here. She was the first woman to make me a tagine, the first woman to give me couscous. She was a special woman, your mum."

"In your culinary education, or in general?" Maddie smiled as she said it.

"Both." My gaze bounced around the walls, strewn with Diane's artwork, as well as family photos of Maddie, Harris, Diane, and Amos. Her dad was significantly absent, echoing his influence on her life. "Is it hard being here without her?"

Maddie took a deep breath. "Sometimes, but I like that Amos is still here, and I love having Mum all around me with her art. I can truly feel her in this room, you know? This was her favourite place, the one where she created stuff. Food, art, poetry."

I glanced down at the kitchen tiles and saw the tell-tale splashes of paint underfoot. No sooner had Diane cleared them up, she'd created another. "I remember it well. Diane painting, cooking, drinking, laughing. She had so much love to give, so much to live for. Fuck cancer, frankly."

Maddie gave me a sad smile. "You can say that all you like, but I think it's still winning." She paused. "I even thought about making that tagine recently, but then I remembered I couldn't chop an onion. I got annoyed with myself then, so I started watching YouTube videos. And you know what?"

"You learned how to chop an onion?"

She shook her head. "No, I learned that people can make chopping an onion seem like such a monumental task. I thought it was just a case of peeling and chopping, but there are specific ways you have to follow so that your fingers don't get chopped off. And I'm quite fond of my fingers, so I didn't want to mess with that."

"Understandably."

"But then, the video kept stopping and I nearly sliced my hand off, so I decided to stick to using my food ordering apps and leave the cooking to the professionals. Everyone has a talent, right? Mine is not cooking."

I laughed. When we'd been together, I'd done all the cooking, or we'd eaten out. "You were always good at baked beans on toast. You added Worcestershire sauce, which shows some kind of cooking ability. Plus, you once made lasagne and we didn't die."

I still remembered that Saturday so vividly it was like it was lasered onto my brain. We'd spent a lazy morning in bed, and had been up for a few hours when Maddie had produced her Italian-inspired opus. It was the only meal she cooked me in the whole time we were together, which is why I remembered it so well. I glanced up at her, my thoughts snagged on that particular memory, a gale of nostalgia ensuring it blew in the breeze. I knew my cheeks had reddened, and when my gaze caught Maddie's, I wondered if she was remembering, too.

The meal wasn't the highlight of that day. We were. The ease of life whenever we were together. Our carefree years.

Being back in this house was bringing them into sharp focus, and it was playing with my mind. Making me think that then was now. Making me think it could happen all over again. I broke our gaze and rolled my neck, not allowing myself to go there.

Maddie didn't move an inch as she spoke. "I've made that meal precisely twice since. I made it for Mum once, and she was amazed. The problem is though, if one person cooks so much better than the other, what's the point in the other one cooking? That's what I found with you, with Mum, with anyone else who's crossed my path since. Even Amos is a better cook than me."

Outside the room, something creaked. Maddie looked up and walked over to the door. "Talk of the devil, sounds like he's up." She disappeared into the hallway, coming back moments later with a very frail-looking Amos. He'd shrunk since I'd last seen him, and looked far older than his years. He could only be around 60, but he looked at least ten years older.

He took a seat almost instantly, before holding out a hand. "Justine. It's been a long time. You're looking well."

I took his hand and sat beside him. His hair was wiry and grey, his skin matching it in colour. He reminded me of an uncle who'd died a similar way: it looked like you could feed Amos every hour for the rest of his life, and he'd still never put on an ounce of weight. His maroon cardigan hung from his shoulders like there was nothing in it.

"Too long, Amos. I'm really sorry you're not well. How are you feeling today?"

He took a deep breath before he spoke, and it rattled

through his body, the sound filling the kitchen. "The same as most days. But it's lovely that you're here. And Maddie, of course. This girl's been an angel since she came back, the living embodiment of her mother. I worry who's going to take care of her when I'm gone."

I blinked, swallowing down hard. Was this the moment where I was going to cry for the first time since Maddie left me?

When I looked up at Maddie, she was biting her lip and I could see she was trying not to do the same. "You're not dead yet, Amos," she told him.

He gave her an exaggerated shrug in return. "I feel like it most days."

I put a hand on his arm and rubbed the pad of my thumb in circles. "You know what, you don't need to worry. Maddie's got plenty of friends who'll be here for her."

He clutched my hand in his, his blue eyes watery. "Including you? I know you've always been special to her, even though she may not always have shown it through her actions."

I put my other hand on top of his and squeezed hard. I cleared my throat and steadied my breathing, sitting up straight. Had Maddie been chatting with Amos? It didn't seem like something that might happen, and yet, life was turning out to be very strange lately. All the things I thought I knew had been turned on their head since James died. Because now, Maddie wasn't the enemy.

When I glanced up, her eyes were glistening, and the

expression on her face told me she wanted to wrap her uncle in cotton wool, to shield him from any more pain.

"Shall we have a cup of tea and you can tell me all about what you've been up to in the past ten years?"

Amos smiled, and even that looked like that hurt. "I'd love that, if you've got time. I know you both lead busy lives."

I looked up at Maddie. "We're in no rush. Put the kettle on. I'll go and get the cake from the car."

Chapter Twenty-One

We left Maddie's mum's house — I couldn't think of it any other way — around an hour later. Maddie made sure Amos was comfortable and had eaten what he could before leaving.

She sat quietly in the passenger seat clutching her documents. I had no idea what was going on in her head, but I realised now her life was far more complex than she'd initially let on. Then, I'd assumed she'd come back to make a quick profit in property.

But now, I saw that coming to James's funeral must have been so hard for her, especially while caring for Amos in his time of need. It shouldn't surprise me, but it did.

The modern version of Maddie had more in common with the one I'd met and fallen in love with all those years ago. She wasn't a cartoon villain, and she certainly wasn't the heartless bitch I'd conjured in my head. This Maddie was exactly the same as the one I'd pictured spending my life with. Which made it all the more odd she'd run off in the first place.

I still had so many questions. Perhaps tonight, now that

it truly felt like I'd peeled back the curtain on her life, I could get some answers.

When we pulled up at the 'car distribution centre' (the car pound to its friends), the sun had long since disappeared from view. However, the air was still warm, carrying heat from the early September day. It reminded of my childhood, going back to school when it was still hot and all I wanted to do was carry on playing.

The pound was set in an industrial park, with a breakdown garage beside it, and an estate of identikit houses facing it across the main road. Beyond that were a few more industrial buildings, and in the distance were once-green fields.

The drive had been fairly quiet. Maddie had preferred to let music fill the air, rather than words. I was down with that. There was plenty of time to talk later.

Maddie jumped out, telling me she'd go and check if her van was here. I watched her walk to the main office, her normal bounce a little jaded. I couldn't imagine what it was like watching another close family member go through what had killed your mum, and I could see she was upset. I hoped some food might perk her up. If we eventually got to the park in Bath to have our picnic before it shut. I checked my watch as Maddie disappeared into the building. At 7:30 pm, it was touch and go, but the food would all keep.

Minutes later, she was striding back to the car, a wry smile on her face. I couldn't tell what that meant. She slammed the door a little too hard as she got back into Kermit. "Sorry, I hate it when people do that."

I shook my head. "No bother. What's the verdict?"

"It's not here yet, but it should be back within an hour." She clicked her tongue before continuing. "So we could either drive off and have a drink somewhere. Or we could have a picnic here. There's a random picnic table over there." Maddie pointed to a beat-up wooden table with benches attached. A classic table that had seen better days. It was nestled against an industrial fence, but it was private. "It's not quite the park opposite my Royal Crescent flat with the sweeping views of Georgian architecture I was anticipating, but it would mean we don't have to come back later or tomorrow."

A loud growl filled the air and I raised an eyebrow. "Was that your stomach?"

She smiled. "It was. It's telling me what I already know: I'm bloody starving. So what do you say? Picnic at the Pound? It at least has the saving grace of having alliterative qualities, even if it doesn't quite have the charm I was going for."

"Picnic at the Pound. Sounds like a straight-to-DVD movie."

* * *

I laughed as Maddie spread out the food, the hilarity of Moroccan hummus, chicken yakitori and an antipasto selection against an industrial backdrop not lost on me.

Luckily, I'd brought fizzy water, as the bottle of red wasn't so welcome now that we both had to drive. We ate for a few minutes, both in need of sustenance, wrung out from the emotion of the day. It barely seemed possible that Gemma and I had completed on a new property this morning. So much had happened since then, it felt like it was a few days rolled into one. Maddie's van, her house, meeting Amos again.

With food doing its work, I was eventually back on more of an even keel. I suspected Maddie was, too. She sat back with a sigh, and my gaze settled on her long fingers, currently battling with the wrapper from a packet of artisan sausage rolls. The packet was winning.

"Amos looks exactly as you said. I wondered if you were exaggerating, but you weren't. How long have they given him?"

She took a deep breath before replying. "A couple of months, but I'm not sure it's going to be that long. You saw him." She gave me a sad smile. "It's just so unfair, you know? I didn't spend enough time with Mum before she died, so I don't want to make that mistake with Amos. But still, it's never enough, is it?" She shook her head. "Sorry. This was meant to be an uplifting evening, and instead here we are, eating amidst a backdrop that looks like it was lifted from an apocalypse movie."

I gave her a bark of laughter for that. "Are we the lesbian superheroes come to save the world?"

"If I'd known, I would have taken better care of my hair

today." She swept a hand through her blonde locks, giving me a grin.

"It looks gorgeous!" Flamboyance flowed through my words. It was true, too. Maddie's hair always looked like she'd stepped out of a salon. Apart from when it had that just-fucked look about it. I vaguely recalled that.

"Thank you." She paused. "And thanks for today, I know it would have meant a lot to Amos that you came in and chatted. Most people don't. I remember it happening with my mum towards the end. People don't know what to say about death, and they certainly don't know what to say to the person who's ill. It's like if they come to the house, they're going to catch dying. I don't blame people, but it's a shame they desert you when you most need them."

I nodded. "It's a societal thing with death, isn't it?"

"It is." She put an elbow on the table and swept away some of the crumbs. "Did you mean what you said to him? That you'll be there for me?"

I swallowed down. "Weirdly, I did. And believe me, that wasn't something I'd planned on saying anytime about you."

"I don't blame you. I've hardly been a rock in your life. But I'd certainly like to carry on being in it again." She looked me direct in the eye. "I never stopped missing you."

Something heavy dropped from my chest and slid down to my navel, before settling there. A slick mixture of heat and emotion, of hearing those words drop from Maddie's lips after all this time. I hadn't been waiting for them, and yet, when they arrived, I felt like I had.

"Then why did you leave? You never told me. I asked you at the funeral, but you just said cold feet. But you don't go out with someone for that long, share what we did, make plans like we did, and then simply disappear."

A lorry carrying a parade of cars turned up, and Maddie glanced up. I turned too, but her van wasn't on there. Back to what we were saying.

Maddie blew out a long breath, her gaze bouncing around the landscape until she settled back on me. She seemed to wrestle with her thoughts and words, chewing on them for a few more seconds before they came tumbling out.

"I know it made no sense, but it did to me at the time. I have a history of catastrophising, as you know. I nearly fucked up my finals. And I ran out on us after a year, didn't I? But you were gracious enough to give me another chance."

"I loved you," I replied. "It's what you do."

She took a deep breath. "I know that now. The pivotal time I ran was to do with my dad. Do you remember I went to see him the weekend before?"

I furrowed my brow. My memory of that time was blurred. I shook my head. "I didn't think you went anywhere until you did."

"I went to see him in his new place. We had a few drinks, and he gave me his relationship wisdom. His twisted, fucked-up relationship wisdom."

I sat back, regarding her. "Your dad. The same one who had so many affairs while he was married to your mother, he could write a whole sodding book about them?"

She nodded. "That one. The one who's still sad, lonely and bitter. It goes to show that if there is a god, he or she has a very warped sense of humour. They kill off my mother who was a saint, and my uncle who's got nothing but good running through his veins. Yet they keep alive my dad, who's a waste of space."

I tried to smile, but I couldn't. Because I couldn't quite believe what I was hearing. "Why did you go to your dad for relationship advice? Isn't he the last person you'd go to?"

"I didn't go to him for that, I'm not stupid." She paused and looked up at me, her cheeks flushing red. "Okay, perhaps I am stupid looking back on it. Or at least, I was. I went to see him because he asked me to. And he wanted some money, of course."

"Did you give him some?"

She nodded. "He was still my dad, and I still had some hope for him back then. He'd started another relationship and I thought it had a chance. I liked his new wife, and they had a child. I wanted to see my half-brother."

This was all news. "You didn't tell me any of this."

She dropped her head, then shook it. "I know, and I'm sorry. I didn't want you to know. Your life was so lovely and simple — loving parents, funny brother. It's what I wanted. But my life wasn't like that."

"Your life was. Your mum made sure of it."

"But everybody said how much I was like my dad, and I guess I took that to heart." She paused. "That weekend, I went to see him, and he was drinking and bitching about his relationship. And I realised then it was him. His relationships failed because of how he was, and it didn't matter who he was with. He'd never be happy in a relationship. He told me to get out of mine. Told me I was like him. Told me not to trap myself in something that was likely to make me miserable."

"And you believed him?"

"I was stupid. I didn't believe him really, not in my heart of hearts, but he sowed the seed of doubt. And we were young. Who knows what would have happened?"

"We weren't getting married. We were moving in together. People do it every single day and most of the world get along with it fine."

"I know. I was overwhelmed with fear. I couldn't tell Mum because she thought he was an idiot. She was right, of course. I couldn't tell you, either. I was so confused. We'd been doing long distance for a while, and I'd survived living on my own. I thought that was a sign. I don't know, I got cold feet and it was inexplicable and inexcusable."

"And then you stopped calling, stopped emailing, stopped everything."

"I can't explain anything about that time. I think I went a bit loopy. Mum was so worried, and I avoided her, too, because I didn't want to answer any questions. That's the thing that really gets me. That I wasted a few precious years I could have been spending with Mum. I wasted them on drinking and on somehow trying to force myself into being more like my dad. Why, I have no idea."

"I really can't believe this is the reason you left me."

"I know. I went to therapy to talk about it a while ago, and she seemed to think perhaps I wanted to feel closer to my dad, and this was my warped way of doing it. Of being more like him. Who knows? Plus my habit of thinking the worst and running. If it helps at all, I could tell the whole time I was speaking to her that she wanted to grab me by my shoulders, stand me up and shake some sense into me."

I wasn't sure how to respond. All this time, I'd put it down to me, to something I'd done. When in fact, it was just circumstance and space. Plus, some weird, random idea Maddie had in her head that she wanted to be like her dad. It was too surreal to even contemplate.

"What about now?" My words came out cold, almost slamming into the warm summer air. But I didn't care.

"Now?" Maddie didn't turn away.

"Yes. Are you still hung up on emulating something that should never be emulated? Or have you moved on to other worthless role models? Who's next? Kim Kardashian? Donald Trump?"

Maddie took a breath before she replied. "Okay, I deserved that. I deserve it all, like I told you. And no, to answer your question, I'm basing my life on other role models these days. Ones that actually did something decent with their lives and didn't go around creating havoc and pain everywhere they went. Like my mum. My nan. Amos."

Her answer was too easy. "Are you still in touch with your dad?"

She shook her head. "No. That ship sailed a while ago when he did the dirty again on Lisa. I'm actually still in touch with her, more so since Mum died. We ran into each other one day and got chatting. I think that was why I wanted to be more like him at that time, because I liked his choice of partner, and that rarely happened. He seemed to like her, seeing as he got married and had a child. But it didn't last, because it couldn't, could it? She's happy now, with a normal bloke."

She swung her leg over the bench so she was sitting side-saddle, before turning to look at me. *Really* look at me. That look I knew so well. Intense. Scorched. Mine. "I'm so sorry for what happened all those years ago, it was all my fault. All of it. None of it was your fault, and I'm sorry I put you through pain."

"You put me through more than pain. You ruined my trust in every relationship I ever had after that. I always thought people were going to leave, and so I pushed them away."

She took my hand, and I let her. I couldn't quite decide if it was the right thing to do or not, but I went with it. "I can't change the past, nobody can. But I can change the future. These past few months, seeing you again, they've been immense. I've never stopped thinking about you, but I knew I didn't have the right to walk back into your life and expect everything to fall back into place. I'd never be that arrogant." She paused, making sure I was listening.

I was.

To every single word.

"And look at you. You're beautiful, smart, sexy and you've done so well with your business. I'm so happy to help you with your next step. But more than that, I'm thrilled to spend time with you, be with you, talk to you." She cast her gaze to the floor, then back up again.

"I've dreamed about your voice so many times in the past decade. It was always one of my favourite sounds. Sometimes in shops I'd hear someone who sounded a bit like you and my heart would almost seize up, wanting it to be you so badly. But it never was." A slight hesitation before she continued. "I knew you lived near Bath, and I've walked around this town so many times looking for you."

"I'm surprised you didn't find me, it's not that big a place."

"Maybe I was scared to." She took my other hand in hers, and cupped them both like they were the most precious things in the world. "But I've found you now, and I don't want to lose you again. Whatever you're prepared to offer, I'll take. Just so you know, I don't expect you to fall back into my arms. I know I fucked up and rebuilding your trust is going to be a gradual thing." Her gaze ran up and down my face, before she took my hand and kissed it gently.

I felt it everywhere, from my head down to my feet. It felt familiar and yet alien. Maddie used to put her lips against my skin all the time once.

But it was all so long ago.

"What do you say? Can we carry on and see where this goes? I want to put things right with you, so we can have a clean slate and move forward." As she spoke, her gaze dropped to my lips and didn't budge.

A whirlwind of emotion battled within me. I'd enjoyed having Maddie back in my life over the past few months, despite my initial misgivings. And yes, there was still a whole lot of push and pull where she was concerned, and I was pretty sure that wasn't going away anytime soon. But moving forward with your life rarely involved going backwards, did it?

What I was also damn sure of was that, where Maddie was concerned, our relationship was never going to be platonic. I knew it now just as I knew it when we met all those years ago in our university bar. That she was someone who was going to play a huge part in my life, and cause me pleasure and pain, which always went hand in hand. At the age of 20, I knew relationships were a gamble. At the age of 34, I still knew.

But it didn't stop my heart pumping so hard, I thought it might explode. It didn't stop a shiver consuming me. And it didn't stop Maddie's lips from being the most prominent feature on her face.

I licked my lips before I replied, staring at hers, glistening in the dusk. "I think we both know we can never just be friends. We're either together or we're not. There's no in-between."

Her lips parted, startled, her cheeks flushed. "I don't want there to be an in-between. I don't want anything between us, Justine. All I want is you."

Chapter Twenty-Two

The following day, in what was soon to be our old studio, Gemma was instructing the class like the pro she was. We had ten students that week, and I'd spent the morning editing our Instagram posts for our Cake Heaven feed, which was the origin of so much of our new business. I was still amazed at how much people loved to watch cakes being decorated, but it seemed like it was an aspirational thing. Some people liked to watch the pros, and others were inspired by it and booked our classes to learn. It was a strategy that worked like a dream. Every week, we posted at least five new videos showing what you could achieve if you put your mind to it.

It was good to concentrate on something that wasn't Maddie, because ever since our impromptu picnic at the pound, she'd been taking up a whole lot of brain space. When I woke up: Maddie. When I put the coffee on: Maddie.

It was almost so easy. Almost. Because ostensibly, she was everything I wanted. But at the back of my mind, there was always the history of us. Sitting and waiting, like a fox about to pounce, tail thudding against the ground. What would people say? More to the point, what would my mother say?

Everyone else seemed to be on-board. But they didn't have so much to lose, did they? They'd never had their heart trampled by her, chewed up and spat out. That's what I couldn't get out of my mind. She'd seemed rational to me last time I'd put all my eggs in her basket.

I glanced up through the half-glass door and smiled as I heard laughter echoing around the studio. I wondered what joke Gemma had just cracked, and thanked my lucky stars I was able to do this for a living. I was in business with my best friend, and it was working like a dream. I had a home, and soon, I might be able to buy a house of my own. I had my health, I had good friends, I had so much in my corner. Could I risk it all on Maddie again? Could I put myself in harm's way and this time, hope it swerved?

Chairs being scraped along the floor signalled it was lunchtime. I waited until everyone had left before I poked my head outside. "Coast clear?"

Gemma looked up from her phone and gave me a grin. "All clear." She put her phone down and went through to the back, coming out with two mugs of coffee. I walked over to sit beside her at the bench. Together, we surveyed the worktops, knowing we'd have to clean this up before everyone came back in an hour. But we were skilled at it, and knew we could execute it in 15 minutes.

I sipped my drink. I didn't really need any more caffeine

this morning. "How was today? Anything interesting happen? How are our amorous ladies?"

Gemma laughed, shaking her head. She'd told me earlier in the week how two of the women seemed to have struck up more than a friendship, and if she were a betting woman, she'd swear they might have gone on a date the night before. "They're being coy, but I think they did go for a drink after class last night. I've caught a few smouldering looks while they were making their American buttercream icing this morning."

"Nothing like buttercream to bring it out of people."

"You know it's true. Perhaps they'll take some home and lick it off each other later."

"You always take it a step too far, you know that?"

Gemma grinned. "You'd be disappointed if I didn't." She ran her finger through some flour on the worktop. "Anyhow, between those two and then the rest of the class discussing rough pregnancies, it's been quite a full-on morning."

"A bit too much oestrogen in the room?" It was a hazard of running a cake school. Too many women in one space always meant conversations about childbirth, marriage, husbands and all the gory details they entailed. Gemma and I often joked we could run a reality TV show from our studio, because all of life was here.

"Far too much this morning. I kept looking at the door hoping Rob would walk in to balance us up a little." She yawned and stretched. "How's your morning been?"

"Productive. I got all the videos done."

Gemma nodded her approval. "Well done. But on a scale of one to ten, how much were you thinking about Maddie the whole time?"

She knew me too well. "I was pretty good this morning, not too much at all."

Gemma raised a single eyebrow.

I laughed. "It's all relative."

"Have you made any decisions on whether or not you're going to let her back into your life as anything more than a friend?"

"Of course I fucking haven't." I dropped my head. "I mean, there is something still there. I think there will always be when it comes to Maddie. But that doesn't mean I have to act on it, does it? I don't do every single little thing based on my feelings. It doesn't work like that. I have to put some rational thought into things."

"Because that's worked really well so far."

I gave her a look. "Can I remind you that you're my best friend. You're meant to be on my side."

Gemma put her arm around me and gave me a squeeze. "I'm always on your side, that's the point of best friends." She squeezed one more time, then jumped up. She grabbed a pen and paper, then sat next to me, scrawling the word 'Maddie' across the top, underlining it three times.

"Okay," she said. "I know you like to write things down, make lists. So let's do that right now." She wrote 'For' on the left side of the page, and 'Against' on the other. Then she made a line down the centre and wrote the number one under the 'For' list. "Give me the first reason why this might be worth a shot."

I tilted my head back up to the ceiling, and then glanced back at Gemma. My mind was blank. I had no idea what should be put in that number one spot.

"I can't think of a single thing. That's a bad sign in itself, isn't it?" I was panicked now.

Gemma rolled her eyes.

I punched her arm. "Stop laughing. Best friend in distress here!"

"Best friend being stupid more like." She sighed. "Okay, I'm going to start you off." Beside the number one, she wrote 'Helped us find new business location'.

I leaned over, picked up the pen, crossed out the word 'location' and wrote 'empire' instead.

Gemma laughed. "Empire it is. Number two?"

I thought for a moment. "She seems genuinely sorry about everything."

"Good." Gemma wrote it down, before glancing up again. "And if it helps at all, Ally says she really is. She told me she always knew of this mythical relationship that Maddie measured all her others against, but she was beginning to think it was made up in her head. But then she met you, and she said Maddie is a different person around you. Like you unlock a part of her that nobody else can."

I frowned. "Ally actually said those words?"

"I might be paraphrasing, but words to that effect."

"Does that mean you're making it up?" This wasn't the time for Gemma to whip up some lies.

She rolled her eyes again. "You're so difficult when it comes to Maddie."

"Can you blame me?"

"No, but I think it might be time to put the past behind you and look forward. Even if nothing happens with her, you'll probably still see her occasionally. The West Country isn't that big of a place, especially when it comes to lesbians."

I knew that was true. I still bumped into exes regularly at any event that happened in the area. If you wanted to find new women, you had to go further afield.

Or perhaps go back to someone you'd met before. Back to nearly-new. Shop-soiled.

"The thing is, Ally did say that. She also said Maddie was never settled in London, and she seems more at home here. This *is* her home, so it makes sense. She also said she's cut up about her uncle, but she's so glad she came home to care for him."

"I know, I saw him the other night. She really loves him."

"So we know she's capable of love." Gemma wrote that down as point three. "She was capable of love before, and she is again. She had a blip. You were a casualty. It happens."

I got up, and walked over to the end of the benches, starting to tidy up as we spoke. "I know that, but I can't just pick up where we left off."

"Nobody's expecting you to. You're both different people with different life experiences." Gemma paused. "And let's be honest: it might work, it might not. But do you want to live your life wondering, 'what if'? I wouldn't. I'd want to have given my all. You owe it to *me* to be happy." She wrote that down at the bottom of the page in a separate list she entitled 'Gemma'.

I leaned over as I passed and pointed at it. "Why have you got your own list?"

"Because I've got to see your sad face every day, and it would be useful to have a happy business partner, not a sad one." She paused. "Plus, seeing as I'm sleeping with Maddie's business partner, it would make a beautiful symmetry and we could double date."

Now it was my turn to roll my eyes. "I didn't think you and Ally went on dates? I thought it was an arrangement." I put the last word in finger brackets. "At least that's what you keep telling me. That you're being all modern and that she's not your funeral bench-warmer."

Gemma cocked her head. "Promise me that's a phrase you only use when it's just the two of us? It should never leave this room, you know that, right?"

"I'm not stupid."

Gemma gave me a grin. "You're not, I know that. I don't have a stupid person as my best friend. But sometimes, when it comes to certain things, you need a little push. A helping hand if you will. And didn't we say at James's funeral we were going to take every opportunity that came our way in a bid to find our chief mourner, our bench warmer?"

I nodded. We had said that. I just never imagined then Maddie could be an option. Tall, beautiful, broken Maddie. As I thought about her, a warm glow settled around my heart. I put down the decorative sails and feathers the students had made and crossed the room. I filled in another line of 'For'.

Gemma walked over and glanced at what I'd written, then back up at me. "I can't believe you wrote that," she said. "Justine, for once in your life, be impulsive. Do the thing, despite not knowing the outcome. Sometimes, you have to take a chance. If you're telling the truth and she makes you feel warm, don't walk away."

I licked my lips. Maybe she was right. All I knew was, every time I *truly* thought about Maddie, I broke out in a serious case of goosebumps mixed with overwhelming want.

It was true. Maddie made me feel it all.

Chapter Twenty-Three

Dean was like a cat on a hot tin roof in the company van on the way over. He was sandwiched between Gemma and I, and about to burst with excitement. It was kinda endearing, and also kinda annoying as he kept jiggling his leg, flicking his foot and generally bothering me.

"Sit still!" I told him. "It's like you're bloody ten years old all over again." He always had been a jiggly little twerp, even as a baby.

"I can't help it. You don't seem to be grasping the magnitude of today. We're going to be on 'Homes Under The Hammer'! National TV. God, I hope it's the blonde presenter and not that bloke with the slicked-back hair."

I grinned. "What about Dion Dublin? You might not fancy him, but he was a pretty nifty footballer in his time."

"I wouldn't mind Dion." He frowned. "But I really hope it's the blonde."

"That makes all of us hoping for the blonde." I plucked my phone from my bag and asked Google for her name. It duly obliged. "Her name's Lucy, for future reference. And slicked-back hair man is called Martin."

"Nobody cares about slicked-back hair man." That was a statement from Dean, not a question.

Outside, the sun was a slice of lemon in the sky, although its rays were more subdued. It'd had a busy summer and was clearly winding down. The van's black plastic dashboard was still hot to touch, though. It was also sparkly, perhaps down to the wedding cake and cupcake deliveries Gemma had made for a friend the day before, where I knew she'd been liberal with the fairy dust. Making cakes for sale wasn't a core part of our business, but it was something we did for a select few. When I touched my finger to the dashboard, it left a mark, but I didn't put my finger in my mouth in case it was dust and not cake debris. You never could be sure.

"Are you nervous?" There was hesitation in Dean's voice now, a slight pause in his excitement.

I patted his knee. "Not yet. When they turn the cameras on, I might have a little wobble. But nerves are all part of it, right? At least, that's what I remember from my year 11 drama classes."

He took a deep breath. "But you're going to do most of the talking, right?"

I laughed. "Yes, me or Gemma. You just need to stand there and look manly. You think you can manage that?"

"Manly is my middle name."

"It's not. It's Gerald. But we don't need to let them know that."

Dean punched me on the arm. "You better not."

"Ow!" I punched him back.

He grabbed me around the waist, going in for his signature killer tickle manoeuvre. In response, I screamed, then wailed, as Dean's laughter also punctured the air. Somewhere mixed in with it I heard Gemma tut, then sigh. But my screaming was louder.

"Children!" No, that was definitely louder. "I'm trying to drive here. You think we can keep the brother-sister bonding until the cameras are trained on you?" She was shouting, but I could hear a smile in her voice.

Dean and I both sat up, his face flushed as I'm sure mine was, too. I glanced at him, and he did the same. When our eyes met, we both burst out laughing again.

I shook my head. It didn't matter how long passed with Dean and I. In the end, we were still the same brother and sister who'd spent their childhood trying to tickle each other to death, or give each other a massive wedgie.

I leaned forward and glanced at Gemma. "Sorry, Mum." I gave her a sheepish smile.

She laughed. "Try to behave. I'll give you both a lollipop when we get there if you do."

"You only had to say." Dean sat up, pulling his shoulders back. "Lollipops work every time."

"He's not even joking," I added.

Gemma pulled into Archer Street and parked outside our new empire, the large windows gleaming in the sunshine.

I gulped: this was it. The start of a new era, the dawning of Cake Heaven, part two. "It looks good, doesn't it?"

Gemma nodded. "It really does. And by the time we're finished, it's going to look immense." She got out of the van and stood on the pavement looking up at our building. Gemma was wearing her just-for-TV outfit of ripped jeans and a black shirt printed with tiny white stars. Coupled with her black-and-white Converse and newly cut hair, she was presenting as the ultimate queer style icon, and I told her so.

"Good." She stepped forward and gave me a hug. "We need to be visible, to represent." She moved her sunglasses up her face. "They need to know we're here, we're queer and we're building fantastic businesses."

I snorted. "Yep we are." I'd opted for blue jeans and a short-sleeved shirt with glasses printed all over it, along with white lace-ups. I'd spent an extra minute polishing my shoes too, in case there was a walking shot. "Let's hope we're advertised as the queer pin-up girls of the auction world. Who knows, we might get some attention next time we're in town, now we're on national TV."

"Paparazzi on our tails, 24/7," Gemma replied with a grin. "What time are the TV people coming?"

I checked my phone. "Half an hour."

"And Maddie's architect?"

"She's due after lunch, so hopefully the TV people should be done by then. They said they'd need a couple of hours."

Maddie and I had exchanged a couple of texts about us using her architect to get some plans drawn up for the new space. We'd skirted around what had happened last week, what she'd said. I didn't want to bring it up on text, it was something that had to be done face to face. Even then, I wasn't sure I'd be able to get the words out. That I wanted to give this a try, that she better not let me down. All the evidence pointed to Maddie living her life like her surname: in a kind manner. I had to believe that would continue.

Because even though it had only been a week since I'd last seen her, I missed her. Somehow, in the space of a few months, Maddie had lodged herself back in my brain and back in my heart.

Clapping broke my thoughts, and I looked up to see Gemma giving me a puzzled look, keys dangling from her fingers. "You ready?"

I nodded, walking over to her. "I'm here, I'm here."

She gave me a look that told me she knew me better. "I need you to be here for this." She grabbed my hand and with her other, put the key in the front door.

"Dean, you ready?" Gemma asked.

To our left, Dean was standing with his phone poised, giving us a thumbs up. "Born ready."

"Smile," Gemma said, fixing me with a look.

I did as I was told.

Dean continued, "In five, four, three, two, one, action."

Gemma gave me a grin, then turned to Dean. "We're here today at the brand-new premises for Cake Heaven in stylish Bristol. This is a whole new chapter of our business, and Justine and I could not be more excited to welcome you through our doors when they open in a few months. In the meantime, book your cake-making course at our website. Link in bio!"

With that Gemma opened the door and we stepped over the threshold, and into our new chapter.

* * *

It was the bloke with the slicked-back hair who turned up for 'Homes Under The Hammer', but he turned out to be lovely, as were the whole team. Dean was a nightmare, fluffing his lines. They kept having to retake the scenes, until eventually, we all agreed Gemma and I would do the talking. By the time we waved them off, Dean was exhausted, the pressure of being manly on camera too much to bear. He left, telling me he had to meet some mates at the pub for 'a football thing'.

Gemma and I had been calm with the crew and Dean there, but when they left and it was just the two of us, we did a little scream. It was probably a good thing the cameras didn't record that. Then we walked around the corner for a coffee and a debrief on our morning.

When we got back, Maddie's architect was waiting — as was Maddie. I hadn't expected to see her, and I was suddenly glad I was looking TV-ready: hair, make-up, outfit, the works.

Gemma glanced at me, silently asking whether or not I'd known she was coming. I gave her a shake of the head before stepping forward and shaking hands with the architect, who was exactly as I imagined an architect would be. She was wearing trousers that were artfully too short, a choppy fringe she could barely see out of, and dark-rimmed glasses that were so big, they almost swallowed her face.

"Lovely to meet you, I'm Justine and this is Gemma. You must be Octavia." I'm normally not that good with names, but I remembered hers. You didn't get many Octavias to the pound in our area.

She nodded, peering at me through her fringe. Did she spend all day pushing it aside? Or was she skilled at dealing with it? "Great to meet you, too. Any friend of Maddie's is a friend of mine." Her accent was straight off Radio 4, but her tone was as warm as the day, and I immediately relaxed in her grip. She was still pumping my hand when I glanced over at Maddie, who was smiling at me hesitantly.

I returned the smile and got my hand back from Octavia. What was Maddie doing here?

"I was chatting to Octavia yesterday, and thought I'd come along to advise her on what I thought about the space," Maddie said, as if reading my mind. "Of course, it's yours and Gemma's decision, but as I know what you're after, I thought it might be helpful."

I nodded. It made sense. "You told me you were crazy busy when we texted." She had. She'd cited her work and her uncle as reasons she couldn't get away. But was it something else, too? Was there a hint of uncertainty in Maddie's eyes?

Maddie gave me a warm smile. "I can spare the time when it's important. You fall into that category."

She thought I was important. I couldn't help the smile that waltzed onto my face or the golden glow that surrounded my heart.

Gemma must have been able to see I was a lost cause, because she took over. "Right, shall we go inside and see what we're dealing with?" Her voice was raised, and it was enough to snag everyone's attention.

Octavia did a little skip, before leading the way. "I can't wait," she said, looking back over her shoulder.

Maddie held out an arm. "After you."

Chapter Twenty-Four

Octavia left an hour later, after inspecting the space fully and making suggestions that none of us had considered. She wanted to knock down a couple of walls and open the whole space up more, which we were on board with. Plus, she had ideas about moving the kitchen, which we had to mull over. I was glad Maddie had invited herself along as she'd been particularly helpful when it came to knowing about worktops, flooring, and lighting.

I could see Gemma was impressed. My best friend kept trying to catch my eye, but I was sticking steadfastly to the script. I was determined that being in the same room as Maddie wasn't going to throw me off what needed to be done today.

However, as soon as Octavia left, something changed. Was it me? I wasn't sure. But suddenly, the day was shaded differently. Gemma was walking around the space unaware.

But I knew.

When Gemma disappeared into the back kitchen with her tape measure, I stared into Maddie's dark eyes, smoky and full of heat.

She looked away. Right then, I knew she felt it too. This thing between us that had ballooned in size as soon as it was just us in the room. As if when it was only Maddie and I, nothing else existed. Just the two of us, with whatever it was between us filling the space, squeezing itself into every nook and crevice.

I let my gaze slide down her flushed cheeks, careful not to flick to her eyes again. It was too risky. Then, there would be too many questions to be answered, too much to say. We'd said we didn't want anything between us. If Gemma left, I doubted there would be.

If Maddie spoke, I'd be drawn to her lips. And if I was drawn to her lips, it wouldn't be her words I'd be thinking about. It would be the weight of her lips. The feel of her lips. How I so wanted them to bruise mine.

Fuck.

Where the hell was Gemma?

I was trying to work out my emotions, but there were too many inside me jostling for attention, conflicted, strained. My heartbeat rose in my chest and lodged in my throat, so much so that when Gemma asked me a question from the back kitchen, I couldn't process her words.

"So what did you think of her plans for this bit?" There was a wall separating Gemma from us. With just Maddie in the same space, I was finding it hard to even blink.

There was a low ambient noise playing in my head. I focused on the door to the back kitchen. Gemma's footsteps sounded, and then she appeared in the doorway, still oblivious, and walked towards me. "I mean, I know we agreed, but was it okay? She said she'd draw up a plan with or without, so I guess we can have a think about it."

Gemma paused in front of me, checking her phone, before looking up.

I nodded. "We've got time. We can talk about it tomorrow at work."

She narrowed her eyes, glancing from me to Maddie, who'd suddenly found the back wall endlessly fascinating. "Okay." She shot me a look, which I ignored. She mouthed something at me, but I couldn't understand it, so I just shook my head.

Not now, Gemma. Not now.

She glanced over at Maddie, checked her phone and stuffed it into her pocket. "Anyway, I've got some shopping to do now the workday is done, so I'm going to leave you two to it." The arch in Gemma's brow was so tall, it could have been installed at Wembley Stadium. She put a hand on her hip and stared at me. "Call me later, okay?"

I barely registered her words, but I nodded. "Will do."

Gemma turned. "See you later, Maddie. Thanks for everything today."

Maddie spun round. "No problem." She watched Gemma walk out, and we both kept our eye on her as she walked along the front of the building.

Then she was gone, and there was nothing to distract us from each other. It was just us. An us that was threatening to engulf us whole.

"Good meeting today." Maddie walked towards me, her every footstep making me shake. I had to concentrate on my breathing. It was something I did every day, every hour, every minute, every second. And yet, with Maddie around, its repetition was in doubt. "It was. Thanks for bringing Octavia. She was brilliant."

"Good name too, right?" She gave me a slow grin, gaining confidence.

She was so fucking beautiful.

"The best. I can tick that off my bucket list. Meet an Octavia. Tick." I took a deep breath. I could totally do this. Have a quick chat, get rid of Maddie, and then have a breakdown. That was totally the way this was going to go. "And your ideas about the flooring and worktops were good, too." I caught her gaze and it was so heated, it almost took my breath away. "Thanks for coming. I didn't know we needed you, but we did." It was almost prophetic.

Maddie took a step closer. "I've helped on this sort of thing before, and I know my flooring. You need something warm, strong and flexible."

I think she was still talking about the flooring. All I knew was her eyes were focused on me, her brows providing the perfect frame, her gaze piercing my skin in a tantalising way. I never thought it was possible to be pierced without pain. Maddie showed me it could be a pleasure.

She was still talking. "Something people will remember. Something that will make them rave about the place. It's all in the detail, and you want to get it right first time."

"You can't always get it right first time, that's the thing." My tone was so scorched with want, it almost burned my throat.

She took another step towards me, not dropping my gaze. I was transfixed by the way the sunlight caught her hair. The way her mouth quirked up at the side, slightly hesitant. The way her jeans were rolled up just so. Precise. Because Maddie had always been that.

"If at first you don't succeed, you can try again. There are no rules. Only the ones you set."

"Or the ones you set?"

She was in front of me now, and I jumped as our hands touched, before she wrapped her fingers around mine.

Maddie shook her head. "I never set any rules. I fucked up. But like I told you last week, I want to make it up to you. I wanted to be your friend, to have you back in my life. But I've realised that I can't be your friend."

I gulped, but my throat was dry.

"When it comes to you, I always wanted to be so much more." Maddie took a further micro-step to me, until her lips were inches from mine. They were hot and inviting, her breath kissing my face. "Tell me you don't feel the same way. Hasn't there always been something between us, something that could never be contained? Something I've spent years trying to put a name to, but I never could. But I think I might know now." She brought my hand to her lips and kissed my knuckles.

The tingle that caused started in my hands, before

zapping through my body, lighting it up until it hit somewhere below my navel.

"All I know is that being around you, staring into your beautiful hazel eyes, and *not* kissing you is getting harder and harder every time I see you." She paused, moving herself right into my space, slicing through the air between us so our bodies were now touching. "It's always been you, Jus." She lowered her face to mine. "Every single person I've ever been out with has never measured up to you. Ever."

She brought her hands up to my face and held it.

Was this the right thing to do? I had no idea. But right now, I couldn't do anything else. In a flash, my flimsy resolve wobbled, then crumbled, like an abandoned sandcastle as the evening tide came in.

Before I knew it, her lips were on mine, and her mouth began to slowly seduce me.

If I'd been wondering how it would feel to kiss Maddie again, I had my answer. It felt achingly right. It felt like the first rays of sunshine in spring. Snow on Christmas Day. There was a lightness to it, and as I kissed her back, I swear I was smiling.

Her kisses were familiar, loaded, certain. I felt strangely vulnerable, but also that this was the right thing to do. This time, it really did feel like Maddie meant it. Her lips slipped over mine like they were made for me.

So many years of what-if, of where was she, of why hadn't she wanted me? But those questions had slowly melted into the background noise of my life, until they faded into bruises, then scars that had become part of my body. Part of my make-up. Part of my DNA.

As the memories of hurt faded, so had the memories of her kiss.

Her touch.

Her.

But now, with Maddie's lips on mine, the memories were springing back to life. Maddie was kissing me and it was everything; her tongue making me melt, her lips making me quake. We kissed with undiluted, unashamed urgency. I completely forgot where we were and who I was. My arms brought her closer, and I wanted *more*. We were in a big space with massive windows. The whole city could see us if they wanted to. But to me, it was just us.

Cocooned.

Cut off.

Maddie and I.

Just like it should be.

My body flooded with a bright sensation and my muscles swooned. Without breaking the kiss, Maddie slipped her hands under my shirt and her touch was almost too much. I did the same, sliding my hands over her soft skin until I reached the waistband of her jeans. My hands brushed against her abdomen and she hissed into my mouth at my touch.

Maddie broke the kiss, her eyes laser focused on me. I gulped again, then stared out at the street, suddenly very aware of the large windows. They were great for baking, but not for privacy.

She followed my gaze, gave me a slow, sexy look that almost made me drop to the floor, before taking my hand and pulling me through to the back kitchen. Once there, she pushed me back against the counter, pinning me there. Her arms were either side of me and I was grateful to be trapped between her and a solid surface because my legs didn't seem to want to hold me up anymore.

She grappled with my shirt buttons, flicking them open and pushing it off. Then she snapped off my bra, her hungry mouth falling on my breasts like they were the first she'd seen in her life. As she sucked and nibbled at me, I threw my head back and gasped, feeling it everywhere. Her tongue and her hands were causing seismic shocks throughout my body, and I knew this was only the beginning. For Maddie and I, the road was wide open. Where we went from here was up to me. But I wasn't looking that far down the road yet. For now, I was going to concentrate on the here and now. The present. On my Kind.

Maddie whipped her top over her head, ridding herself of her bra, too. I pulsed anew. I pulled her to me, kissing her skin, marvelling at how perfect she was.

But I wasn't allowed to for long. Before I knew it, Maddie's hands were on my crisp jeans, tearing open the zip, a zeal and urgency to her movements. Then her hands returned to my breasts, my back, before slipping inside my jeans, and then my pants. I swayed against her but she held me firm. Our gazes caught for a moment, as she yanked down my remaining clothes, and I stepped out of them. We were at the point of no return, and it hovered above us. My chest heaved as we paused.

Maddie's fingers were so close to their target, her breath hot on my lips.

Now was not the time to stop and ask questions. Now was the time for action. For finishing what we'd started. For doing what had always come so naturally to us.

The talking could wait.

Maddie paused for another moment, getting the permission she needed from my heated stare. If she was in any doubt, I thrust my hips forward, forcing her fingers nearer. Then I moved my lips to her lobe.

"I want you," I whispered, my voice barely crawling from my lips and into her ear.

She didn't need telling twice. Maddie wasted no time pressing her lips to mine, her body following suit. Maddie's finger slipped through my wetness, and I cried out. I couldn't help it. Maddie was inside me and it felt like I'd won the jackpot. I shuddered.

She slipped another finger in, groaning into my mouth as she did, the vibration sending shockwaves spiralling through me.

"You feel so good." She curled into me as I thrust forward.

We stopped then, revelling in this moment, one I never thought would grace my world again. It was one of those times you wish you could ink into your memory. Tattooed in place, time-stamped forever. One movement would mean this moment was gone. And I, of all people, knew you couldn't hold on. You could pause and take it in, but then you had to move forward and live your life. Because the future held the promise of so many more moments, ones just like this, and those moments might be even better. That's what I had to believe, especially with Maddie.

I couldn't try to recapture our past. I didn't want to. I had to let go and trust that what came next would be better. So in that moment, I relaxed my muscles and then my mind. I let go. I gave myself to Maddie.

She was all-consuming now, physically and mentally. Her free hand squeezed my nipple as her fingers skilfully worked me, slipping in and out, her thumb circling my clit. So much sensation, so much Maddie. It was overwhelming.

Her thrusts took me higher, her tongue on my neck. Syrupy pleasure heated low in my pelvis and spread through my limbs. I felt woozy with lust, high as a kite. We were lost in each other, insulated from the outside world. I gave a guttural moan as my orgasm began to roar within me, heat thrusting to all my nerve endings.

As muscles danced and my orgasm boomed, I clung to Maddie, remembering how steady she could be. At one time, she was my rock, my world. Right now, she was all that was in my sightline as I came all over her fingers, digging my nails into her back, groaning into the air. She thrust some more until I stopped her, and then I rode out some aftershocks, before coming back into the here and now.

My eyelids flickered open and I looked up into her smile.

I didn't have to say anything. I knew what she was thinking. It was written in the upturn of her mouth, in the heat of her stare. Then her lips were on mine again, before she pulled back. "I've been wanting to do that ever since I saw your gorgeous face again." She paused, and kissed me again.

She was still inside. I never wanted her to leave. "You said you didn't want anything between us." I dropped my gaze to her lips, and my eyelids fluttered shut briefly. "You got your wish."

She smiled, squeezing my butt cheek with her free hand. "I got the first part, that's true. But I want more. I don't want this to be a one-off. I want to make everything up to you, Justine. All of it. I want to prove to you that I'm worthy of your time. Your attention. And if you'll let me, your love."

With my orgasm still booming in my ears, I stared at her. Fuck, she had a way with words, whereas I could hardly string a sentence together. Not right then.

The sound of a muffled phone ring broke the spell, and Maddie sighed, wincing. "That's Ally's ringtone, and she only uses it when she has to. She normally messages me." She straightened up, taking her hand with her. I breathed out, putting my head on her shoulder.

For now, she stayed where she was.

The phone ringing stopped, and then began again. Maddie's breathing stalled, and then she opened her eyes, her grey stare looking direct into mine. "Sorry, I can't ignore her twice. That's her code if it's urgent, to call again right away."

She squeezed my butt cheek with her hand, then slowly moved backwards and grabbed her T-shirt from the floor where it had been discarded. She shrugged it over her head before she returned the call. Before the material covered her stomach, I marvelled again at her flat abdomen, her firm muscles I'd recently run my fingers over. Physical work clearly suited Maddie and was what kept her in such great shape.

I heard the call connect, saw Maddie nod her head, and then she disappeared out the door and back into the main space.

I breathed out for what seemed like the first time in days. My blood was still sprinting around my body, and my thoughts were jumbled as I pulled myself upright. That's when I realised I was quite naked. I glanced down to see my knickers on the floor. I took a moment to be amazed. Because this was amazing. Incredible. And also, highly improbable.

I'd been so sure nothing would happen, until the moment where it had become inevitable. When Gemma had left, the heat had risen and nothing else in the world but Maddie's hands on my body and Maddie's lips covering mine would do. Nothing but that would calm the surging desire that stampeded through me, a desire that was still raging, if I was honest.

Next door, Maddie's voice was stretched, pained. Whatever Ally wanted her for, it didn't sound good. Somehow, I knew I wasn't going to get my hands on Maddie now. If I was five, I would wail and gnash my teeth at the injustice, but I wasn't. Despite all evidence to the contrary — and the fact I was standing naked in my new business premises — I was in fact an impressive business owner in her 30s.

I glanced down at myself, and then, feeling exposed, stepped into my knickers and pulled them up. Then I found my bra and shirt and dragged it on, my fingers still shaky and useless. Desire hummed in me like a car waiting at a kerb, its engine still on. Damn it, I wanted to kiss Maddie into next week, then fuck her until she got that look on her face, the one I still remembered. The one I'd love to see again in real life. And then I'd like Maddie to do exactly the same to me.

To what end, though? Where was this going? Maddie had said she wanted more, but could she be trusted? I pushed those thoughts aside. For the past hour, I'd decided to live in a fantasy land where actions had no consequences and no emotional ties. For now, I had to treat this as a promising start, and think about the rest later.

My head was heavy with whirling emotion as I pulled on my jeans. I couldn't see properly through the tangle of my hair as I leaned over and I swept it away from my face.

Moments later, Maddie strode towards me with purpose. Her hands slid into my pants once again, squeezing my butt cheek, making me whimper. I was putty in her hands.

"Fuck, I want you." Her eyes blazed as they focused on me, and I had no doubt her words were true. But then she withdrew her hand, zipped me up and fixed the buttons on my shirt. They were one out.

I grinned, aware I was still unsteady on my feet. "I want you, too."

"But I'm afraid I've got to go."

I let out an audible groan, reaching around and pulling her to me. "I don't want you to leave." I didn't know much in that moment, but I knew that. I wanted to drown in Maddie, safely ensconced in my make-believe world.

"I don't either." She bruised my mouth with another scorching kiss, before pulling back, eyeing me. "But that was Ally, and we've had a disaster at the Bath site. The upstairs neighbour's ceiling has collapsed, and there's been a huge leak." She paused. "We can only hope the wall's collapsed, too, to get around the planning issues." A wry smile. "So I have to go, and I've never been sorrier. This was incredible, just so you're in no doubt." She lifted my fingers to her mouth and kissed them. "I hope we can pick this up again very soon?"

I gazed up at her, caught in her trap. "I hope so, too," I whispered, before kissing her lips again. "Message me, okay?"

Maddie gave me one last kiss, before walking through to the main space.

I followed her, and watched as she gathered up her keys and her bag.

"You need a lift back?"

I shook my head. "Nope. I told Gemma I'd measure up for a few things and I haven't done it yet. I've been somewhat distracted."

Maddie's mouth quirked at that.

"Plus, the walk will do me good. Lots to process — in the business and otherwise."

She nodded. "There is." A pause. "But I'll speak to you soon, I promise."

I gave her a grin, trying not to think about Maddie's promises to me before, promises that had never come true.

Chapter Twenty-Five

The next day, I had a family Sunday planned: lunch with my parents, brother, and grandad. The house looked gorgeous as I approached, its front garden filled with yellow and pink roses. I swung open the white wooden gate and headed down the side of the house to the back door, as always.

Mum gave me a hug as I swept into the kitchen, and I wondered if she could tell. If she knew that I'd let Maddie in yesterday. Truly let Maddie in. Had I done the right thing? As soon as I'd stepped out the door of the new Cake Heaven, the make-believe land I'd constructed had imploded, and then it was just me. Feeling as naked as I had when I was stood inside, with Maddie's tongue in my mouth, her fingers buried inside me.

My vision wobbled as I recalled it all, and my clit twitched. She was too good, that was the problem. We were too good. The connection we'd always had was still there.

Last night, Maddie had sent a text telling me she had to stick around the flat to get the repairs done; it was worse than she'd anticipated. She also had to spend time with Amos, who was having a bad weekend. She couldn't see me today, but had said she'd call later. It wasn't a signpost to our future, but at least she'd texted. For now, it was enough.

"Cup of tea?" Mum was already putting the kettle on as she asked, and I nodded. I could really do with something stronger, but it seemed a little churlish to ask before lunch. I knew the face Mum would pull.

"That'd be great." I sat at her kitchen table and stared out into the garden, which was a similar size to Kerry's garden. That instantly took me back to where Maddie and I had our first chat after the funeral. The chat where the walls had come down a little, and the keys to our world, the one we'd once inhabited, had been dangled in front of my eyes. What had she said then? That she'd got cold feet? It was more than that I now knew. But if she'd done it once, was she capable of doing it again?

Whatever, I couldn't get Maddie out of my head. She was like a recurring soundtrack, stuck on repeat. The feel of her. The taste of her. Yesterday afternoon, while brief, had been the next tantalising glimpse into what might be, and I wanted to see more.

"Dean was around here last night waxing on about the TV and telling us he's going to be a star. Is it true or is he making it all up?" Mum sat opposite me at the dining table, wearing a smile that told me she already knew the answer.

"Let's just say he's a better builder than TV star."

She gave me a smile. "He's good at that — you've seen our extension." My parents had a side extension done a few years ago, all by Dean's fair hands. It was still standing. We were still impressed.

"Where's Dad and Granddad? I don't hear the TV."

"Dad's down the pub — a football thing. He took Granddad with him, although Granddad wasn't happy about it. Claims he can't hear what people are saying. But he could do with getting out of the house, so your dad insisted."

I smiled. "Is Dean down there, too?"

"I think so." Mum tilted her head. "He was also telling us about Gemma and Maddie, and how much Maddie's helped you out with getting the new building." She paused. "You never really mentioned it before."

I shrugged like it meant nothing. But even as I did, I knew Mum would see through it. She'd known me all my life, and seen all my previous highs and lows, after all. So, I decided to dip my toe in the Maddie water, just to test her reaction.

"I know what you think about her, and you're right. She did leave me and I am being careful around her." I swallowed down my lies to see how they tasted. Palatable. "But when it comes to our business and helping us find a new place, she's been invaluable. I was resistant at first, but we've spent time together since and talked about the past."

Mum gave me her measured face, the one that said as far as Maddie was concerned, she wasn't yet in or out.

She was still considering. "Dean said she knew what she was doing. Whatever happens, I don't want both of my children falling in love with her again, because that's what happened last time. I hoped it would end well for at least you back then, but it didn't. I don't want her coming in again, ruffling feathers and leaving."

I rolled my tongue over my bottom teeth. "She didn't ruffle feathers. We were together for nearly four years."

"I know that. But she still ruffled feathers all the same. And that was me being nice, by the way."

I turned my gaze to the floor, before bringing it back up to Mum. I didn't blame her for being sceptical. Why wouldn't she be? "She seems different this time. Or at least, back to how she used to be. She's helping Kerry with the soon-to-be-baby, she's looking after her uncle, and more importantly, she explained things to me. Why she left."

"And did she say why she came back? That's my worry. Not just to fill your head with ideas again?"

I shook my head. "Business, but also family. She's caring for her sick uncle and working here. She hadn't even planned to get back in touch with me, but James dying threw us together."

Mum said nothing for a few moments. "Just be careful. I can hear it in your voice there's more to this than you're saying." She locked my gaze with hers and I could feel my cheeks heating. "I don't know if anything's gone on already, and I don't want to know." She put a hand on my arm. "You're still my little girl. I don't want you to be hurt again."

"I know that. But I'm also a grown woman and you're going to have to trust me on this. Whatever I decide."

Of all the people I had to tell, it was Mum I was most hesitant about. Which is why I didn't want to spill anything before I knew what was going on with Maddie. I didn't need her judgement. My own judge and jury were already the harshest people I knew.

"I trust you. It's her I'm still wary of." She squeezed my arm. "But we're your family and we're right behind you whatever you do, you know that."

"Even if it involves Maddie?"

Mum's mouth twitched, before she nodded her head. "Yes, if she's who you choose, then even her."

"Good." I put a hand on Mum's arm. "I can't predict the future, but it might involve her. And if it does, you might be seeing her again. Her mum died a couple of years ago, and her uncle's terminal. She might need some familial steadiness in her life soon."

Mum was about to reply when Dean walked in, followed by Dad and Granddad.

"Well if it isn't my favourite granddaughter come to see me!" Granddad came over and hugged me, the smell of beer wafting from him. He seemed to be shrinking every time I saw him, and he was getting thinner, too. Mum had said he'd started to lose his appetite, apparently something that happened as you aged. His blue eyes were still radiant, though, surrounded by bunches of soft wrinkles.

"Hello, Granddad. How was the pub?"

"Noisy." He took his jacket off slowly, and took it out to the hallway to hang it up.

Dad came over and gave me a hug. "Hello, love. Dean's been telling us both my children are TV stars. I can't wait to see it."

I gave Dean a look. He was shameless.

Chapter Twenty-Six

Monday morning and I was back teaching a three-day class I'd taught dozens of times. For that, I was grateful. My teaching was on auto-pilot as I went through the motions of how to make decorative flowers for the top of your cakes, and how to ice a cake with ultra-precision. By the end of the day, every one of the ten students would have something they were proud of and amazed by, even if they'd doubted themselves at the start. Learning to decorate cakes was like learning any new skill: just keep going, keep trying and eventually you'd get there.

Was that the case with Maddie, too?

I'd got home the night before around eight, and settled down with a glass of wine to watch the Sunday night film: 'Notting Hill'. If I was feeling discombobulated with Maddie back in my life, it was nothing that a glass of Malbec and a dose of Julia Roberts couldn't cure. I'd often thought they should put films like 'Notting Hill' on prescription for illnesses, both mental and physical. Feeling down? Watch a rom-com. Broken your leg? Watch a rom-com. They might not mend bones, but they did wonders for your mood.

I'd put my phone on charge in my bedroom so I wouldn't be tempted to check it all night long. When I retrieved it, there'd been nothing. She hadn't called and she hadn't messaged. I wasn't asking for much: just a text. Sure, Maddie's emotions were being split in all different directions: business, family, me. I got that. But didn't I warrant a single message?

It was the complete opposite in my heart. Where Maddie was concerned, I'd turned my emotions off at the mains all those years ago, and then ignored them for years. But now she was back, I'd turned the switch again, and they were all surging in one direction. It didn't feel like they were being reciprocated.

I knew it wasn't like last time, that we were both in different places. I knew Maddie had a lot to deal with. But it didn't stop it from feeling *exactly* the same. Like time had stood still, and Maddie was always going to let me down, and go radio silent.

"Justine?"

Resha, a student, had one arm raised and a frown on her face. I walked over to where she was having issues curling the delicate petals of her icing rose. She hadn't cut into the initial shape enough, so she didn't have enough flexibility in the petal now. Cake decorating was all about laying the groundwork and getting every step right from the beginning.

It was hard not to let my mind wander to Maddie when it was conjuring thoughts like that. I'd done the right thing with her, or so I'd thought. I'd kept my distance, let her back in gradually, even sorted out the past. So why did I feel so naked in the present? Why did I feel like Resha's rose petal? Like something was off, the measurements not quite right?

Hours later I saw my class off, and started the big clear-up with Amisha. I'd drunk too much coffee and was jittery, which was doing nothing for my mood. I should be kinder to myself. Gemma had phoned to say she was coming over to take me for a coffee after work, which was weird for a Monday. Amisha was whistling an off-key tune, and I needed a moment to myself. I slipped into the loo and locked the door.

It was all going to work out, I had to believe that.

However, as I sat, I heard a splash. I stood up and saw my phone had fallen from my back pocket into the water, sat at the bottom of the bowl. So now, even if I wanted to will Maddie to text me, it was never going to work. As I fished my phone out, I wasn't sure whether to laugh or cry. That just about summed up my luck since Saturday. Hot sex, followed by a single text, then the cold fingers of doubt.

How I hated the cold fingers of doubt.

They were able to grip me like no other.

I walked out into the main space, where Gemma was

leaning against a workbench, chatting to Amisha. When she saw me, she gave me a grin.

"There you are. We thought you'd fallen down the loo."

I held up my phone. "I didn't, but my phone did."

Gemma gave a snort. "Was it in your back pocket again?"

I nodded. "Now even if Maddie is trying to text me, I won't know. Which about completes my transformation back to the stuttering idiot of ten years ago."

Gemma walked over and put her arm around my shoulders. "I believe we've had this conversation before, and the answer to that is not quite." She paused. "And even if you were, you're far better dressed than back then. Remember that time when you thought dungarees needed to make a comeback?"

I stuck my tongue out, smiling despite myself. Gemma could always make me smile.

She glanced around the workspace. "Another successful batch of clients learned how to make flowers again today?" The students had left their floral creations on the metal shelving to the left of the door. Tomorrow, we'd make the cakes they were going to adorn, and on the last day, they'd ice and decorate them to perfection.

I nodded. "Nobody died, and we achieved peak floral decorative heights, didn't we?" That last bit was directed at Amisha, who nodded.

"We couldn't have got any higher," she replied, before disappearing into the back office with some paperwork.

I don't know what we did to deserve Amisha, but I thanked my lucky stars for her every day.

I looked up at Gemma, who had her concerned face on. "Are you okay? I know this weekend has thrown you. It's zigged and then it's zagged."

"You mean having sex with my ex and then her disappearing again? That's a whole lot of zigging, right there."

Gemma held up her phone. "I just had a text from Ally."

"Great. She's texting you, but Maddie is ignoring me."

"They're still both at the other property that's having issues — the one Dean's working on — and their Bath flat sounds like a nightmare. They had to wait for someone from National Heritage or whatever it's called today. Sounds like a right pain in the arse." Gemma paused. "Has she been ignoring you completely? No texts at all?"

I shook my head. "She sent one on Saturday, but nothing since."

Gemma sighed. "She might be trying to text your dead phone now. Cut her some slack. She only ran off because there was an emergency. Plus, she's dealing with her uncle."

I harrumphed. "I'll try. It's just pressing a few buttons for me. Ones I'd thought were dead and buried."

Gemma put a hand out and touched my arm. "It's a different time and you're both different people. Just try to remember that, okay? In the meantime, I'll text Ally and let her know. Maddie can communicate through me. Now, are you coming for a coffee?"

Chapter Twenty-Seven

Gemma left soon after buying me a coffee. I decided to stay back and sort through the mountain of paperwork that needed to be trimmed before we moved. If I was going to be miserable, I may as well put it to good use.

It was gone 8:00 pm when I heard a banging on the door outside. We'd had issues with drunk passers-by getting lairy with our front glass, trying to lick the cakes through it. This was a little early for that. Plus, it normally happened on a weekend, not Monday night.

I sighed, the tweak in my groin reminding me of the sex I'd had two days ago. Sex that was probably never going to happen again, despite Maddie's words. As I opened my office door and walked into the main space, I wondered if we had any wine in the office fridge. Wine was called for tonight.

But that thought fled my mind as soon as I glanced up and saw who was making the noise and banging on the glass in the now-dark evening.

Maddie.

When our gazes locked, she gave me a tired smile and pointed at the door handle.

In my excitement to open it, I cracked my hip on a workbench, and staggered the last few metres to the door, opening it with a grimace.

"Hi." All the speeches I'd semi-started in my head disappeared when I breathed in her aroma. Eau de Maddie. They should bottle it and sell it to me, their audience of one.

She wasted no time sliding inside, closing the door and pulling out a stool, before sitting me on it. "Are you okay? That look like it hurt."

"Because it did." I lit up inside. She was concerned about me. All was not lost.

"Sorry to be the cause of your hurt." When she said those words, her gaze was on me, soft and true. "And I'm sorry for going silent since Saturday. It wasn't my intention. But I figured I should tell you that in person." She took my hands in hers, stepping forward before kissing them. "I'm still here, in case you were wondering. Just drowning in a sea of rubble and family illness."

The feel of her lips on my skin took away any pain. That was all I needed. A reconnection. A sign this was going the right way. I was glad Maddie had realised that.

I brought my gaze to her face. "I had been wondering. You fuck me, then you leave. It was a little familiar."

She winced. "I know, and I'm sorry. But with the roof, then the other property, and Amos on top, I've struggled to catch my breath. And then I was texting you to see if you were free, but Ally told me you lost your phone."

I gave her a sad smile. "I dropped it down the loo. Kinda sums up my day."

She stepped forward, her arms snaking around me. "I hope me turning up has made your day better."

"Infinitely."

Her lips met mine, writing me an instant apology. Her warmth enveloped me, tumbled down me till I was lost in it. The pain in my hip was a long distant memory. The pain in my groin, however, was reignited. I smiled into Maddie's lips.

When we pulled back moments later, her eyes were on me. "God, I missed you. I missed this."

"I missed returning the favour and fucking you on Saturday." I pulled her closer, as near as she could get. There were already too many obstacles between us. Any that were in my power, I was going to obliterate.

"Not as much as I did." Her grin lit up her eyes. I loved her smile. I always had.

She pushed back some of my fair hair from my face. "Are you growing your hair, by the way? It's getting long. I like it."

I shook my head. "I hate it. I've just had other things on my mind than going to the hairdressers. Moving my empire. Putting my heart on the line with a certain someone."

She squeezed my waist and kissed my lips again.

My heart skipped a beat.

"I've told you, I'm not playing around, despite circumstance conspiring against me." She pulled back, her gaze pinning me in place. "Did Ally tell you what happened with the other place? The one Dean's working on?"

I gave her a vague nod. "I know it's not good. I know you've been up against it."

She exhaled. "We have. Plus, Amos isn't good. At all. I don't know how much longer he has." She took a deep breath, before checking her watch.

"In fact, I can't stay long. I told him I'd be home tonight to watch a show with him. An episode of 'Murder She Wrote'. He's been recording them all. He used to watch them with Mum, but now Harris and I are the stand-ins." She pursed her lips. "So this is a flying visit. Just to let you know you've been on my mind, in between juggling family and building chaos."

I shook my head. "I get it, and thank you for coming over. I was just sitting in my office fearing the worst."

She shook her head. "If it seems like that, I'm sorry. Maybe by the weekend, we can have more time." She glanced around. "Much as it was spontaneous, the next time we have sex, I'd like it to be somewhere more comfortable than your work."

I laughed. "Me, too. Although the new building is now forever stamped."

Maddie grinned, holding up a palm. "I'm not complaining."

"Good to hear." I took a deep breath, then stilled as our eyes met. I stared into Maddie's grey depths, the windows to her heart. They were wide open, ready for me to march in.

I ran my thumb over her knuckles.

She had to go, I could feel her pulling away.

She leaned over to the door. "Just checking the van hasn't been towed again." She gave me a wry smile. "I promise, once things settle down, you'll be my number one priority."

Warmth and relief gurgled in my stomach. Maddie was being forthright, honest.

"Can I ask one thing?"

"Anything."

"Keep in touch, okay? I'm getting a new phone tomorrow, it should be the same number."

She kissed my lips. "I promise."

Chapter Twenty-Eight

Monday's swift visit had done wonders for my mood. However, despite me getting a new phone, Maddie had gone silent again over the past few days. Just one text, saying she was snowed under again, and that was it. Our connection on Saturday was in the rear-view mirror; Maddie's Monday night kisses seemed a long way off. Everything we'd said and done, with the promise of more.

Had it been too much, too soon? I didn't think so. However, if she was that easily distracted, perhaps I was better off without her. Four days and one text? I didn't need more of her mind-fuckery to mess with my life. She'd done that once, and I'd be damned if I was going to let her do it again.

Perhaps Mum and her warnings had been right all along. Why were mums always right? Perhaps without her own, Maddie was lost for guidance. But because of her silence, I had no idea what Maddie was feeling.

I crashed through the door of Rob's bakery and slumped at the counter. When he saw me, he gave me a puzzled look and leaned on his elbows, bringing our faces close together before we spoke.

"Jus."

"Hmmm?"

"Why are you still wearing your Cake Heaven apron? You never keep that on." His coffee machine hissed as he heated some milk.

I looked down and saw he was right. I shrugged. "My mind is elsewhere."

"You haven't even been teaching today, have you? I thought I only saw Gemma through the window."

He was right. Gemma was front of house today, but I'd put an apron on to keep my clothes clean while I cleared more of the back office in preparation for our move. I was pushing Maddie to the back of my mind by throwing myself into a task, and it had at least resulted in a decluttered office, which was a kind of win. However, it hadn't erased my mind of Maddie. There was no eternal sunshine or spotless mind in this tale.

"Can I have a coffee or do I have to have an inquisition first?" I wasn't in the mood.

Rob raised an eyebrow. "Inquisition? You wouldn't have lasted ten minutes on the Spanish Armada, believe me." He set the coffee he was making on the counter. "Sit down, I'll bring it over. Even if this is your third cup of the day, which is how I know things are serious. I remember when your mum had that cancer scare. That was a five-cup day." He paused, panic flitting across his face. "Your mum's okay, isn't she?"

I sighed. "She's fine. This time it's me."

He looked even more alarmed.

"Nothing to do with cancer. To do with women."

He exhaled a long breath. "Okay."

Five minutes later, I was sat with a coffee and a slice of Millionaire Shortbread, Rob staring at me through narrowed eyes. "She's definitely got your new number? You're sure of that?"

I nodded. "It's the same number, just a different phone. She texted on Wednesday to tell me she was snowed under. One text since Monday, though. It's now Friday." I exhaled, my shoulders slumping. "She told me this was important to her, that we were important. But she's not acting like it is. She's not doing anything that tells me what happened between us meant something."

Rob paused. "What happened? You haven't told me. Did you kiss?"

A burning rose in my cheeks as Rob's gaze stayed on me.

"More than kiss?"

I gave him a slow nod, closing my eyes briefly as the memories assaulted my brain. I could still feel it everywhere.

"Okaaaaaaaaay." Rob clicked his tongue against the roof of his mouth. I could tell he was thinking. Then he covered my hand with his. "Have you got your car today?"

I shook my head. "It's getting serviced. I got the train."

"Come home with me tonight. Is she still at the Royal Crescent flat she's doing up?"

I frowned. "Last I heard Gemma say, she was there with Ally. I think."

"That's just around the corner from me. Get the flat number, and we'll go and find her. What do you think? There might be nothing to worry about, but it's best to see her face to face."

A million thoughts whizzed through my mind, most of them downers. But Rob had a point. Perhaps going to Maddie was the easiest thing to do. She'd come to me on Monday. Now, on Friday, it was my turn to return the favour.

I sat up straight in my chair. "I can ask Gemma if she knows the number. What time do you leave?"

* * *

Rob's car always smelled of bread, which I loved. Bread always calmed me down, eating it and smelling it.

"Did I tell you that Jeremy saw her the other day? Maddie, that is."

"He did? Where?" He'd got my interest now. Jeremy had seen Maddie and Rob hadn't told me? I was about to chew him out, but then I realised he didn't know I'd slept with her. I'd been keeping that information close to my chest, on a need-to-know basis.

"In the Co-Op. She was buying bananas and Celebrations, apparently."

"All the major food groups." I stared ahead as Rob swung his red work van around Queen Square with its grass still not recovered from the hot summer, and up the hill to the Circus, grand Georgian houses lining either side.

This had been a spur-of-the-moment decision. However, now faced with the prospect of seeing Maddie, I wasn't sure what I should say. Perhaps I didn't need to say anything. Perhaps we just needed to be breathing the same air. When I could see the whites of her eyes, I'd know what she was thinking. At least, I hoped I would.

We swept into the Royal Crescent, the van jolting along the cobbles. This was an address that never failed to impress. A semi-circle of 30 multi-storied terraced houses, its Georgian architecture was Grade I listed and one of the most visited attractions in the area. It sat atop the city, already stuffed full of Georgian grandeur. However, this was still Bath's premier address.

Most of the terraces had been sliced up into flats, but a couple still remained as huge houses. All of the doors were painted black with chrome fixtures and fittings. Black railings paraded the entire length of the houses, and the low light of the evening stretched out and reclined on the lawns opposite. I'd always loved this crescent as a student, but knowing Maddie was here now, my feelings were tangled.

I pushed my knotted insides down as I told Rob where to park. I took a deep breath as he drew up outside the flat Maddie was doing up. The lights were off, which wasn't a good sign, but I still had to try. I turned to Rob, hoping I was giving him a face that said 'this doesn't matter much', even though I could feel my body rooting to the spot, my legs filling with lead.

"I'll wait for you."

I shook my head. "You don't have to."

"I know."

My hand shook as I slammed his door, then pushed open Maddie's gate, which squeaked as I did. I gathered myself, took a deep breath and raised my hand, my knuckles sounding like cannonballs being fired as they rattled the solid wood.

Nothing. My heart galloped in my chest. I clenched my right hand into a fist as I knocked again. The third knock didn't connect as the door was wrenched open. Ally stood on the other side.

"Justine!" Something passed over her face, but I couldn't tell exactly what. I didn't know her well enough yet. "What are you doing here?"

"I came to find Maddie."

She sucked on her top lip. "She's not here. I only just got here myself an hour ago."

I stared at her. If Maddie hadn't been busy here, then where the hell was she? My stomach fizzed with anguish, and a familiar feeling of despair flushed through me. "You've no idea where she is?"

Ally hesitated, before nodding. "Amos isn't doing so well, so she called this morning to let me know she wouldn't be here. I think she planned to let you know, too, but maybe the day ran away from her. It sounded like she wanted some alone time, so I left her to it."

My despair morphed into worry.

I gave Ally a sharp nod, then swivelled and ran back to the car. "Thanks, Ally!" I shouted over my shoulder, as I skidded in front of Rob's van, then opened the door and slid into the passenger seat.

"I know we only just came from there, but Maddie's at home in Bristol. You think you could drive me back if I smile at you sweetly?" I gave him my best smile, the one that always worked with Gemma. I wasn't sure Rob was such a pushover normally, but today, he was on my side.

"Just for you." He gave me his mobile. "But can you message Jeremy and tell him you're making me drive back to Bristol, so I'll be late home?"

* * *

All the same memories of the past washed over me as I arrived at Maddie's place. I tried not to glance up at her bedroom window and remember everything. I failed.

"You don't have to wait this time." I leaned over and kissed Rob's cheek. "Thank you for doing this, though."

He nodded. "No problem. You're going to be okay?"

I unclicked my seatbelt. "I guess I'm about to find out."

My second knock on a door I expected to find Maddie behind was far less fraught, because I had an inkling of what to expect. However, the fear etched into Maddie's face when she opened the door was far more than I anticipated.

Plus, she didn't open the door wide. Before I even got any words out, she was shaking her head.

"Hi." Her voice was a whisper, sadness echoing through it. Even her normally styled eyebrows were in disarray. Tiredness seeped from her body. She looked exhausted.

"Hi. I went around to the flat in Bath and Ally told me you were here. Don't be mad at her, I was just worried about you."

Maddie nodded, but wouldn't make full eye contact with me. "I'm sorry about all this. About being off-grid. Stuff has snowballed this week, and I know my timing's not great. It wasn't what I expected to happen."

I reached out and covered her fingers with mine. When our skin connected, I jolted, but Maddie stepped back. I couldn't read her today, not like Saturday or Monday. Now, her eyes were clouded over, her stare vacant. "How's Amos? Can I help? I'd like to."

She gripped the door, shaking her head. "Don't take this the wrong way, but no. He's not good and I have to focus on him at the moment. I can't think about anything else, I hope you understand."

I gave her a slow nod. "Of course. But I can help. You don't have to do this alone."

She swallowed, then took a deep breath. "The doctors have said he hasn't got long, so I need to give him all my attention, to be fully present. I'm sorry if that's not what you want to hear, but it's what I need to do. If you're here, I'll feel guilty about not being with you." She looked up, her eyes sparkling with emotion. She was holding so much in. About us. About Amos. About her mum.

"I won't be in your way, I promise. Let me help you, Maddie." I wanted her to know she had back-up.

But Maddie was still shaking her head. She always was stubborn. I should know this by now.

"I'm sorry, Jus. I can't do us as well. Amos is in his final days, and I'm spending them by his side. Right where I should have been for Mum." She gave me a crumpled smile, took a step back and pushed the door a little more closed. "I'll call you, I promise, but for now, I need to be with Amos."

She wasn't going to let me help, was she? In desperation, I put a foot in the door as she tried to close it. She looked at me again, her face flushed.

"If you're not going to let me help, can I at least just give you a hug before I go? Just so you know you're not in this alone?"

Maddie took in a deep breath, considered this for a moment, before giving me the faintest nod, and opening the door.

I stepped forward and wrapped my arms around her, rubbing my hand up and down her back. I wanted her to know I cared about her, about us. That what we'd started wasn't just about us two, it was about her whole life. If that involved her family, it involved me, too.

Maddie was stiff at first, resisting my help. Still running, even when she was in my arms. However, after a few strokes of her back, I put my lips to her cheek and kissed her. When I did that, her whole body softened, and she melted into me, her hands wrapping around my waist.

"I've got you." I squeezed her tight to demonstrate.

When she pulled back moments later, she was wiping tears from her cheeks, shaking her head. My own emotions were a bubbling cauldron inside me, but still no tears had spilled out. When it came to tears, I was barren.

Maddie took a deep breath, refocusing on me.

"Are you sure you don't want me to stay? I can make you tea?"

She smiled, then shook her head. "I need to do this alone. Just me and Amos."

I backed away. At least she knew I was here. And at least now, I got why she'd gone radio silence. After her mum, this was a huge deal. "Just promise you'll call me if you need anything. Anything at all, okay?"

"I will. I promise."

The door clicked shut in my face and I was left standing on the pavement in her Bristol street, alone, the early autumn air tickling my face.

Chapter Twenty-Nine

I'd had one text from Maddie since I went to her house on Friday, thanking me for coming to check on her. I was giving her space to be with Amos; I knew it was important. However, showing up on Saturday to the new Cake Heaven was still a jolt to my system.

Here was the next stage in our growth, where it should all fall into place. This was the place Maddie had found for us, the place Kerry had helped us buy, the spot where we could make all our dreams come true.

What a difference a week made. This time last week, Maddie had fucked me here. Now, she was unnecessarily facing a crisis on her own. All I could do was let it play out and be there to pick up the pieces when she needed me. Gemma had told me to hang in there. I was doing my best. But with Maddie on hold, it was time to get cracking with the rest of my life.

My new phone beeped in my pocket. It sounded like a frog croaking. I needed to change that, but hadn't got around to it yet. I pulled it out of my pocket to see a text from Mum asking if I wanted to come for dinner tonight. I said no. I couldn't face her today.

"Justine!" Dean's sing-song voice broke through my mental veneer. "What did you want on these walls?" He slammed the wall to his left.

"You've got the plans." I walked over to him. "We're getting rid of this and making this the main wall." I pointed down the side. "And shelves with a peg board all along here, okay?"

Dean nodded. "I had it upside down." He waved the plans at me and gave me a grin. "Is that Octavia coming later?"

"Think so."

He stared at me. "Cool. I liked her, she was a bit of alright."

I gave him a look. "A bit of alright? Have you time-travelled back to the 1970s?" Dean had met Octavia at Maddie's other project, and had expressed his delight to me already over the phone.

That's when my brother blushed. Actually blushed. I took a step back. "Do you *like* Octavia?"

His cheeks were now the colour of aubergines. "I think she's cool. She's not the sort of chick I'd normally go for, but she was interesting. We had a right old chat about lighting in buildings, which, as you know, I'm a big fan of."

Well, well. Dean and Octavia was a pairing I wouldn't have put together in a hurry. "And are you going to pursue it?"

He shrugged, tucking his chin into his shoulder. "Might do. We'll see. I don't want to fuck up this bit of the build. Maybe wait a bit, see how things go."

I was impressed. My brother didn't want to put us in jeopardy just so he could score with Octavia. Perhaps I sold him a bit short at times.

"I like her plans, anyway. She's hot and clever. Just the way I like my women." He gave me a wink, then strolled through to the back, studying the plans as he went.

I glanced up as I heard footsteps approaching: Ally had come in, and was smiling at me. "Just thought I'd come to say good luck in your new venture." She gave me a hug, and I thought again how weird this was. Maddie had found us this place, yet she wasn't here.

"Thank you. We're excited to get started." But my tone didn't sound that excited. "Have you heard from Maddie at all? I'm worried about her."

Ally nodded. "No change as far as I know. Amos is hanging in there. She's dealing with it in her own way, which is to shut herself off from everyone else. It's not healthy, but that's how she does things." She gave me a tight-lipped smile. "It doesn't mean she doesn't want to see you, though. She's going through so many emotions."

I shook my head. I knew how hard it must be for Maddie. "I just want to help. I would have happily made dinner or just been there for her. But she wouldn't let me in when I went around."

Ally sighed. "She did that to me, too. It all goes back to

her mum dying. She still blames herself for not being there, and now, she doesn't want to miss a beat with her uncle. She doesn't quite realise she can lean on her friends, too."

I folded my arms. "Perhaps we need to stage an intervention. Show her helping means she can focus on her uncle, while we focus on her."

Ally put a hand to her chin. "I've been thinking the same thing. How about we go over there tomorrow? I agree with you, she can't do it all on her own."

"Great idea." Relief spread through me. If we went together, Maddie was far less likely to turn us away. I gave her a hug. I had a lot of time for Ally. When I pulled back, I flicked my head towards the back kitchen. "The main reason you came is in the back kitchen discussing plans with Dean if you want to see her."

Ally gave me a grin and walked that way.

Chapter Thirty

The following lunchtime, I had a warm feeling in my chest. I wasn't sure what it was, but it felt hopeful, which was more than had happened in previous days. Ally was coming to pick me up in the afternoon and we were driving over to see Maddie. Action was always better than inaction, and this felt like we'd be doing *something*.

Maddie needed to see she had friends who cared about her. Ex-lovers who cared about her. A possible current lover who'd put herself out there, and now was just looking for a little something in return. Hell, I didn't want to have sex with her and a massive heart-to-heart. All I wanted was to offer her some support. Make her tea and a sandwich. Give her a hug. The simple stuff that made a difference.

I walked into my kitchen, with its warm orange tiles and breakfast bar, and made myself a coffee. I looked out at my small back garden. It had crossed my mind that I might have to think about moving to Bristol if the business really took off and demanded more of my time and attention. Seeing as I was only renting this place, I could leave — but it would be a wrench. I'd lived here for the past eight years, and it was the first home I'd made on my own. My first post-Maddie house. The one where I'd learned to be me again. Now I was standing in my kitchen, my life on hold because of her once more.

What was she thinking this morning? How was her uncle doing? My heart swelled as I thought about her. Was she freaking out? Having second thoughts about us? I had no idea.

My phone beeping interrupted my thoughts. I picked it up. Maddie. Was everything okay? My stomach rolled as I clicked for more.

'I'm so sorry Justine. About it all. Mx'.

I blinked, as my mind went into meltdown. What did that mean? What the hell was she sorry about? I paced the kitchen, my blood pumping faster, my face set to grimace. My relaxed Sunday had just been tipped out the window. Fucking hell, Maddie was maddening.

She was sorry about it all. Sorry we'd slept together? Sorry we'd met again? It didn't make any sense at all. I wasn't that bad at reading people, was I? However, it wasn't just me. Everyone agreed that Maddie was a good person doing good things these days. Everyone but my mum.

Before I could jump off the roof of my life, my phone began to ring. Maybe it was Maddie explaining herself. I checked the screen. Nope. It was Gemma.

"Hey you." I tried to sound jaunty, even though I was anything but. If my emotions were a boxer, they were on the ropes, clinging on for dear life. Why was Maddie sorry?

"Hey yourself," she replied.

Gemma's sharp intake of breath told me this wasn't a breezy social call.

"What's wrong?" Wasn't it weird how you could sense a tone from someone's breath?

"It's Maddie. Her uncle died yesterday, and she just texted Ally to say she's leaving."

If my heart could have vaulted out of my body and raced out the front door, it would have. "Leaving? Where the fuck's she going?"

At least now her text message made a little more sense. Not the sense I wanted, but still.

"We don't know. We're on our way over to the house, but she messaged Ally this morning. She spoke to her briefly, and she was frantic, saying she had to get out of her house, that it was cursed, that she'd seen far too much death in it."

That was something I could totally understand. "But if he's only just died, where's she going? There's so much to sort out. The funeral. The house. Her uncle's stuff. Plus, she's got work commitments. She can't just up and leave." I wanted to say she had emotional commitments, too. But did she? Maybe not.

"I know. She can't go for good now, but she was talking about it, saying this place has too many bad memories and she didn't know why she'd come back."

"Fuck." Sometimes, you didn't need many words to sum up how things were going.

"She's not thinking straight right now, that much is clear. Ally wanted to let you know, but she was also wondering if you might know where she's gone? She said she had to get away for a couple of days, but is there anywhere she might be? A favourite place you might know about that we don't? Friends? Family? Somewhere she might go to think?"

I was already running into my bedroom to get dressed, my brain whirring with possibility. Where could she be? At her brother's house? Too obvious. At The Spanish Station? Maybe for a drink. Even back in London? Perhaps.

"I'll make a few calls and check out the bar we love first. She told me she went to The Spanish Station after her mum died."

"Great. We're heading to her house because she said she left a key with a neighbour. We're going in to see how things are, clean up if it needs it. Just to make things a little better for when she gets back."

"Thanks Gem, that's really sweet."

"It's for you, too."

My heart lurched one more time as, snagging the phone between my cheek and shoulder, I grabbed my jeans from the bedroom floor. "I know. Call me if you find her, okay?"

* * *

I drove to The Spanish Station, killed the engine and sprinted across the car park. The day was drizzly, and I'd grabbed my light rain jacket for the first time in what seemed like ages. I'd also had to turn my windscreen wipers on, which seemed like a novelty. There had just been a light rain shower and the air was thick with the smell of wet tarmac. It was probably too early for Maddie to be here, but it was worth a shot.

I skidded around the corner to the front of the bar, the beer barrels and their stools wet from the rain. I peered inside. Maddie wasn't there.

My heart dropped like an anchor, clanking in the pit of my stomach. I'd been almost sure this was where I would find her, that she'd be waiting for me to walk around the corner and take her in my arms. But she wasn't.

Perhaps I didn't know her like I thought. Perhaps she didn't want to be saved.

It started to rain again, indicative of my mood. I flipped up my grey hood and trudged back to my car, the spring gone from my step, disappointment weighing down my limbs. I began a text to Maddie, the latest of five I'd sent in the past hour, telling her I was at our bar and she wasn't here. But then I deleted it. If she wasn't here, I didn't want her to think I was such a sap. Shit, getting tangled up again with anyone was hard. Getting tangled up with my first love was crippling.

I fished in my jacket pocket for my keys, diving into Kermit to get out of the rain. I threw my phone onto the passenger seat, taking my hood down and staring at myself in my visor mirror.

I still hadn't cried. Throughout this whole week, even though I'd been through a gamut of emotions, I still hadn't shed a single tear. What was wrong with me? I gave myself a stern look. Perhaps the facts would unleash something. Crying was emotion leaking out. It was just like physics, right?

Maddie's uncle had died.

I had no idea where Maddie was.

My future with her, which I'd been beginning to imagine, had gone up in flames.

I closed my eyes and concentrated hard. Maddie was gone. She was sorry. I screwed up my face. I strained.

Still nothing.

Although if I wanted to do a good impression of someone on the loo or being a bit mad in their car, I was doing a valiant job.

I shook my head, gave myself another look in the mirror, then swallowed some saliva. I needed to focus. *Really try.*

I exhaled, dipped my head, closed my eyes and got a mantra going in my mind: 'She's gone. Maddie's left. That's it.' I breathed in and out quickly, my heartbeat speeding up in my chest.

Cry, dammit.

The sound of my phone ringing split the air. My eyelids sprang open, and I grabbed it, annoyed at the interruption. But then I saw it was Kerry. Who never called me. Shit, was Kerry going into labour early?

I pressed the green button. "Hey, you okay?"

"No," came the instant reply.

"Is it the baby?" My heart was sprinting again.

"I'm only eight months, the baby is still firmly in my stomach." She paused. "However, I have a very distraught Maddie on my sofa, and I think she'd like to see you. She might not admit it, and she'll kill me for saying it, but I think she would."

Relief swept through me and I wanted to punch the air. "She came to you."

Of course she'd gone to Kerry.

"She did. It makes sense, doesn't it? She's been visiting a lot, talking about grief. So when her uncle died, she knew I was a safe spot. Someone who understands. Someone who's dealt with what she's dealing with now."

It did make sense. My emotions were on a carnival ride, and I had no idea where they were going next. I was glad I'd located Maddie, angry at her for running, but I had a feeling that was from years ago. But the fact Maddie had run to a safe place, to our friend, to someone who understood?

I might be a little hurt she didn't come to me, but I understood. If anyone got grief, it was Kerry.

I started the car. "I'm on my way. Do you need anything?"

"Just your smiling face." She paused. "And chocolate is always a good option."

Which made me smile. "Consider it done."

Chapter Thirty-One

If I'd had any anger towards Maddie, there was no way I could keep it going when I saw her curled on Kerry's sofa. She was still the woman I'd begun to entertain visions of a future with. But today, above it all, she was broken; I could tell at a glance it was going to take some time before she was put back together again. What's more, that was only going to happen if we managed to convince her to stay put, where her friends were. *Where I was.*

Maddie wasn't the only one who looked beaten up by the experience. Kerry's face was puffy, too. It was only just over five months since James died, plus she was almost ready to drop. She gave me a hug, then offered me a tea, before disappearing into the kitchen. She turned the radio on, then up. She didn't reappear straight away, which I assumed was my cue to deal with Maddie. It was what I was there for, after all.

I sat next to her and put my arm around her, putting my nose against her cheek.

Maddie inhaled a large breath as I did so.

"I'm so sorry about your uncle." The bags around her

eyes needed scaffolding, and her skin was pale and watery. I got the impression she hadn't long stopped crying, and she blew her nose before replying.

"Thanks." She pulled back, eyeing me warily. "Sorry I haven't been in touch. It just got too much."

I took her hand in mine, giving it a squeeze. "It's okay, it's done now. But I should let Ally and Gemma know where you are. They're up at your place giving it a spruce up."

Maddie didn't reply, just settled her gaze on me, before looking away.

"How are you feeling?"

Maddie coughed. "Probably like how I look. Like my world's just fallen apart. I don't know how Kerry's been coping as well as she has. It's the worst. It's like," she put her hand to her chest, "it's like losing Mum all over again. Same house, same disease. Fuck cancer." She closed her eyes and sat back.

"I'm so sorry, I know it can't be easy. The opposite of easy, in fact." I was struggling for words to fit her pain, but I ploughed on. "I went to the dock to look for you. When we all weren't sure where you were, I thought you might have gone there."

A flicker of a smile crossed her face. "I thought about it, but then decided I might be tempted to throw myself in the dock rather than contemplate life. Plus, I associate that place with you, with happier times. I know I went there after Mum, but I don't want it associated with death too much."

"It might have made you feel better."

She shook her head. "I don't think much is going to make me feel better. I don't think going there and having a drink would help anyone." She paused, before looking up at me through her long, dark lashes. "Although you being here is having some effect." She shook her head. "I don't deserve you, though. I'm sorry about everything. I know I haven't handled it well."

"It doesn't matter." I had to say that, even though it did. All of it mattered. Maddie had run away once before, and she was threatening to do it again. That was the biggest fucking deal of all. But her thinking was tainted with grief. I got that. I hoped that was all it was.

"It kinda does. I want to explain."

I took a deep breath. "Okay, then. Explain it to me."

She sat up, rubbing her face with both palms before addressing me. "For starters... I didn't want to jinx whatever was going on between us. I didn't want us to start again in a rocky time. It feels like that's where we left it, and I wanted to bring positive things to your life, not complicate it. If we're giving this a go, I want it to be as perfect as it can be."

I shook my head, holding her gaze. "You're stupid, you know that? Life's not like that; it's not perfect and it never goes to plan. I know that, and you should know that, too."

Her chest heaved as she sat back, covering her face with both hands. "I can't believe he's gone. My last link of that generation. I think I was kinda hoping there might be a miracle and he might survive, but I knew the chances were stacked against him. But now, it's just me and Harris."

"Plus you've got a ton of friends who are here to help. Including Kerry and me."

She nodded, wiping a tear from her cheek. "I know, it's just hard."

I took her in my arms and she let me, her body gently throbbing as sobs echoed through her. When she pulled away some moments later, I knew I'd have a wet patch on my shoulder, but I didn't care. All I cared about was being there for Maddie. Death was a great leveller. It melted all the other stuff away, and just left you with the moment, the here and now.

But there was still the elephant in the room. I was going to address it. "Ally said you were talking about leaving. Were you being serious? Is that what you meant in your text when you said you were sorry?" My heart clattered in my chest as I waited for her answer.

She dipped her head, before taking a deep breath. "I don't know. Yes. No. Maybe." She sighed again. "Being here is messing with my head. On the one hand, there's you, Kerry, Rob, everyone. It's been great getting back in touch, it really has. But this is also where my mum died, and now where Amos died. If I stay in that house, what's next? How long until I get cancer and die?"

I shook my head. "It doesn't work like that." I gave her a tired smile. "This is you running away. Your default. But how about accepting the help being offered by everyone? Plus, we've only just got together again. I thought we were heading somewhere." My lip shook as I spoke, and I glanced at her. "Isn't that what you thought, after last Saturday?"

She glanced up, exhaling. "Of course. But I didn't know if I'd blown my chances this week. Why would you want to be connected to me? I'm the kiss of death. That's another reason why I was thinking about leaving. Being here and knowing me is dangerous. I'm like the black widow, cursing everyone who comes anywhere near me."

"Now you're just being ridiculous." I took her hands in mine, staring into her eyes, making sure I had her full attention. "Listen to me. Last week was big. I hope you felt it, too. I don't do stuff like that, and it wasn't just with anyone. It was with *you*." I leaned in and kissed her lips. "You're my first love, and I could fall back in love with you. It might take time, it might need work, but I'm willing to give it a go. But to do that, you have to be here." I leaned in closer. "Promise me, you're going nowhere?"

She drew in a shaky breath, then nodded. "I promise."

I kissed her lips and she clung to me, before there was a noise in the room and we sprang apart.

"I hope you're talking some sense into her." That was Kerry coming in with a tray of tea and biscuits — the British cure for everything. "I swear, if she starts going on about being the kiss of death to everyone around her again, I might scream. You've just had some bad luck, that's all.

I mean, serious bad luck. But you're not the only person who has bad luck. I have." She pointed at her belly. "This little person has, and he or she isn't even born. He or she will never know what an amazing man their father was."

Kerry sat down, blowing her nose. "But if you're going to stay around for anyone apart from yourself, think about the people in this room. I know Justine wants you to stay, for reasons that have always been obvious. You two are meant for each other, and the sooner you both wake up to that, the better."

Maddie and I looked at each other, eyes wide, but said nothing. It didn't feel like Kerry was finished yet. She wasn't.

"The other reasons you should stay is for me and this little one who's going to be here before you know it. I want my child to be surrounded by people who will tell them about James, about what a guy he was. I also want them to be surrounded by lovely people, solid friends of mine. You two both fall into that category."

She wagged a finger at Maddie. "Plus, I've enjoyed you being back in my life, and I don't want you disappearing again, never mind Justine will be terminally miserable if you do." She put a hand to her forehead. "So please, can we stop all this talk about you leaving and just settle on the fact that you're staying, and we're all going to be here for you?"

She stared at us both, and then I turned to Maddie. "I couldn't have put it better myself."

Satisfied she'd said her piece, Kerry sat forward. "Now, who's for tea and a chocolate digestive?"

Finally, Maddie cracked a smile. "If I'm staying, I better have a biscuit, hadn't I?"

Chapter Thirty-Two

I knocked on the door of Maddie's place. I was trying to think of it as 'Maddie's place' and not 'her Mum's house', and I was encouraging her to do the same. Since Amos died a few days ago, Maddie had been staying over with Kerry because she didn't want to sleep in this house alone. Kerry had called to ask if I could intervene. She said Maddie needed to go home and get back to normality. Kerry of all people knew it was essential that Maddie got over her fear. My plan today was to get Maddie to stay put. I was happy to stay, too, if she needed me.

She answered and gave me a hug, before stepping back to let me through. We'd done nothing more than hug since our chat after Amos died. I knew that incredible sex had happened, that layered emotion had been dredged up. However, I wasn't going to push anything before Maddie was ready. I was just happy she was letting me back in to her life and her house.

I walked through to the kitchen, still my favourite room in the house, and sat down at the table while she put the kettle on. Maddie smiled at the box I set down.

"You brought cake?"

I nodded. "A bit obvious, but cake always makes things better."

"True. Thanks." She clutched the worktop behind her. With her height and her blonde hair, she looked so like her mum, it almost took my breath away. She belonged in this house, and she belonged in this kitchen. She just had to start believing it.

"The last of Amos's stuff went this morning, to a homeless charity down the road. Loads of clothes and shoes they can use, so that's good. Plus all his gadgets, which he loved. I thought about keeping them, but I like the thought of him living on through others. They were thrilled with his iPad and his laptop."

"I bet they were. That's a lovely thought — him living on through others."

She nodded. "We got a date for the funeral, too. October 14th. That'll be over three weeks since he died. Can you believe it takes nearly a month to bury someone in this country? In Spain they do it within a day or two. Seems weird we keep people hanging on so long." She paused, turning to get the mugs as the kettle boiled. "But anyway, it's done."

"You're doing really well, I hope you know that. Going back to work, sorting Amos's stuff and his funeral."

"Kerry helped, too. She's been great, knowing what to do. And Harris has been around a lot as well. We both organised Mum's funeral, so we remember that. But Kerry has been amazing. And Gemma messaged to say she was doing a funeral cake. I think she wants to make that a new trend, so you can make some money out of it."

I laughed. "She always was the more entrepreneurial of the two of us." I glanced at her as she sat down with the tea. "Your funeral cake is on the house, though."

"You won't get rich with that business mindset." She locked eyes with me, taking a deep breath. "Thanks."

"I love this kitchen, have I mentioned that?" The light was flooding in, and I could almost taste her mum's essence in the air. "I hope you love it, too. I know you haven't stayed here since Amos died."

She bit her lip. "It's just a bit weird. But I know I have to."

I reached across the table and wrapped my fingers around hers. "You're not doing this alone, remember?"

"I know." She brought my knuckles to her lips and gently kissed them.

For the first time since we had sex at our new empire, I felt like I was allowed to experience my feelings. Allowed to look her in the eye like *that*. Allowed to feel like I wanted her again. I tried to say something to that effect, but I couldn't quite find the words. Perhaps it wasn't quite the moment just yet. I swallowed and looked at her.

"I still don't know if I can live here, though."

My heart almost stopped beating. I sat back, my jaw fixed tight. "I thought you'd decided to stay?"

She nodded. "I have, but just in this area, not in this

house. There are so many memories here, I can still sense Mum and Amos. Plus, there's Harris to think of. He needs the money, and if we sell, he can have his share."

Okay, she wasn't *totally* leaving. The hairs on my body danced as relief lathered my skin. "Don't just sell up because Harris needs the money. You could buy him out, couldn't you?" I was pretty sure she could, but I had no real idea about her finances.

She nodded. "I could. But if I'm going to start again, maybe it would be better to do it with a clean slate, somewhere fresh?"

I shook my head. "I disagree. I love this house, I always have. This is the house your mum bought when she got independent, so it has good vibes. And yes, I know she also died here, and so did your uncle, but think of that as a plus point. They'll always be here, be around to watch over you, and that's a very precious thing.

"If you sell, you'll be losing a bit of both of them. They're in the bones of this house, just as you are. This is your chance not to run away from the past, from your family history. To change your pattern of the past, and lean in to your history. To embrace it."

She stared at me, her eyes so bright, it felt like there was an extra light behind them. "You make a very convincing argument. Have you ever thought about going into motivational speaking?"

I laughed. "I only get passionate about things I truly believe in. And I believe in you and your family. It's your decision, and whatever you decide, I'll respect it." I paused. "But do you want me in your life?"

Maddie sat up reaching both hands across the table, taking my hands in hers. "You know I do. And the other day, you said you did, too. I want a future with you, Justine. I thought I'd made that clear."

"Nothing's very clear when you keep talking about leaving and giving me a heart attack."

She dropped her head, before nodding slowly. "I get that. It probably feels like I'm blowing hot and cold. But really, it's just me talking out loud, trying to figure things out. Figure out if I can stay in this house or not."

That made sense. Even if it was bloody annoying.

Maddie gave me an apologetic grin.

"To me, it's simple." I dropped her hands, waving one arm through the air. "This house holds happy childhood memories for you. Plus, if you want me in your life, wouldn't you rather I was able to walk into this kitchen and be instantly happy?"

Maddie snorted. "How about I sell the house to you? Sounds like you love it more than me."

"You love it, too, and I wouldn't buy it. Half the reason I love it is because it belongs to you. So long as you keep it, that will continue. That counts for a lot, so don't throw it away."

She took a deep breath in and I could see her eyes glistening. "You think I should?"

My heartbeat was thundering in my ears. "I really do.

You promised me the other day you'd stay. Now promise that you'll stay *here* and face life head-on. Starting tonight, staying here to sleep."

"The only way I can do that is if you stay with me, too." Maddie's cheeks were flushed, her eyes dark.

"I brought my toothbrush." I stood up and held out both hands. "I'm not going anywhere."

She looked me in the eye. "I'm not sure what I've done to deserve another chance with you, but I'm not going to fuck it up again, I promise." She was already getting up as she spoke.

"You've made a lot of promises before. Is this one you're going to keep? The next time something bad happens, do you promise not to shut me out?" Our eyes locked, and I shook as her hands squeezed mine. Maddie's old promises were paper thin. I needed them to be thicker now, to carry more weight. I needed it now more than ever before.

"You don't have to worry anymore. You want me to embrace my future?" She stepped forward and wrapped her arms around me. "I'm doing it now. I promise, you'll never have to doubt me again. I'm never going to give you a reason to do so."

* * *

Maddie's mouth was on mine in seconds, and I felt like I was on a fairground ride, my feelings whooping in my head. Maddie had promised me everything, and I was starting to believe.

We moved into the hallway and staggered up the stairs, me clawing at her clothing, and Maddie swaying like she was drunk. She wasn't. It was just that we'd been talking around everything for so long now, we'd run out of words. Maddie was staying. For now, that was all I needed to know.

Because underneath it all, there was us. The heartbeat of us that had never stopped beating, even though it had been in intensive care for so many years. But I'd never stopped thinking about Maddie. Never stopped dreaming about 'what if'. Now, 'what if' held out her hand and pulled me into her arms, before we stumbled through her doorway and tumbled onto her bed, both of us laughing.

I remembered then. Being with Maddie like this had always been effortless. Never once jagged. Intimately, we'd always been explosive. Being with her, I was able to be myself completely: to laugh, to relax, to stare into her eyes with naked ambition. Like I was doing now. My ambition was to love her like she'd never been loved before. To make her feel safe. To get over everything that had gone before. When we'd met again, it was her that had to work to make me feel safe. Now, with so much loss in her life, the tables had turned.

The first way I was going to do that was to get us connected, skin on skin. "I've wanted to touch you so much, ever since the other Saturday. I've ached to be inside you."

She groaned. "I've wanted that, too."

I put a finger to her lips. "Then let's make it happen." I saw the acquiesce in her eyes as she watched me kneel up beside her, before reaching down and pulling off her top. Damn, she was beautiful. Flat, strong abs, defined biceps, smooth skin.

"Are you sure you haven't been working out? You make me look a bit flimsy."

She grinned up at me. "No weights were harmed in the making of these muscles. It's what happens when you have to cart planks of wood, tiles and bathroom suites around all the time. Are you impressed?" She raised up on her elbow, and flexed her right bicep.

I pulled her up and snapped off her bra. "Nothing turns me on like talk of planks and tiles." I stripped off my clothes, shucked Maddie's bottom half, and when we were both naked, I lowered my body onto hers. It drew low groans from both of us. A decade had passed since the last time we did this. In some ways, it seemed like no time; and yet, it seemed like a lifetime. But now she was underneath me, I was calm, assured.

But it wasn't like before, far from it. This was us, but a new us.

I kissed Maddie's cheekbones, down her long neck, along her collarbone. Some things, I remembered. When I licked her there, she looked down, startled. But when our gazes connected, realisation dawned on her face. I knew what she liked. At least, what she used to like.

"That hasn't changed?"

She bit her lip, her eyes thick with emotion. "No."

I took in her small, rounded breasts, the pebble of her

nipple, lingering with my tongue on its curves and dips. I wanted to taste every last bit of her. To remember, but also, to be delighted by the new. Maddie's body hadn't changed much on the outside, but the inside was a completely different story. My job was to join the dots, to make her whole self sing. I was determined to do it.

I flipped her over, and nibbled my way from the nape of her neck to her bum cheeks, taking special care there as she wriggled beneath me. When I left a lasting mark on one of her cheeks, she groaned underneath me, which made me lie the length of her, put my mouth next to her ear.

"You still like that?"

Maddie groaned. "Yes."

It was all I needed. I wanted to test out some of the other things I remembered about her. Her love of straddling my mouth, for instance. As I rolled her over and lay beneath her, I tapped my chest with one hand.

Her eyes grew darker as she rocked on my hips. "You remember more than you let on." She reached down and kissed me, leaving her lips inches from mine, her breath hot on my face. "I always remember how good you were at this. I've never done this particular thing with anyone else."

An arrow of lust landed in my core. "I better make sure it's as good as you remember then."

Maddie gave me a long, hard look, followed by a final bruising kiss. Then she moved herself upwards, until her pussy was over my mouth.

I grabbed her butt cheeks and took it from there. As my

tongue began to explore her, Maddie breathed out. So did I. I worked up to touching her clit, revelling in the feel of her, of wanting to make this unforgettable. Had she really stopped doing this because of me? If that were true, what else had she stopped doing, too? Had she put a lid on a part of herself after me, just like I had when she left all those years ago? It seemed like we'd both been waiting for permission to be ourselves fully again.

I was determined to fuse us back together in that moment, starting with a sweep of my tongue up and over Maddie's hot centre; once, twice, three times. She was so wet and ready. I pressed into her with wild abandon.

Maddie writhed on top of me, her butt cheeks clenching in my hands. "Oh Justine, yes!"

I knew she was close. With one last arch of my tongue, one last squeeze of her cheek, I made her soar, and she fell forward over me, gasping for breath, her body shaking. I grinned into her, only stopping when she told me to. After a few moments, I guided her down, laying her on her back, before kissing her lips gently, then sliding two fingers into her. She was so wet.

I kissed her again, and as Maddie's eyelids fluttered open, I began to fuck her slowly, curling into her, the air thick with emotion. Right there, something slotted into place, like a puzzle piece I'd been searching for.

All along, it had been Maddie.

As my thumb connected with her clit once more, Maddie stilled. Then her hands dug into me. As I built my rhythm, she cried out again, shuddering as she came, clutching my body and my heart.

When her orgasm faded, I kissed her cheek, then her neck, before coming back up to meet her eyes. What I saw there almost made me cry.

Almost.

"You don't know how much I've missed you."

I gave her a knowing smile. "I think I do." I moved my fingers inside her.

She closed her eyes and breathed out. "Do you have anywhere to go this afternoon?"

I shook my head.

She gave me the widest grin I'd seen in a while. "Good. I've got some plans if you're interested."

I went to reply, but was cut off by Maddie's lips crushing against mine.

Chapter Thirty-Three

Amos's funeral was on a dark autumnal day in mid-October. As we drove into the car park, I couldn't help but get flashbacks to James's funeral. To the change in weather. To the fact that life went on, despite what the chief mourners might think at the time.

Maddie had insisted I drive Kerry, so she was in the front seat next to me. Maddie and Harris were in the funeral car, which was somewhere behind us. My stomach lurched as we pulled up, and I looked across at Kerry, her bump huge, her face stoic. As I killed the engine, I took her hand in mine and looked her in the eye.

"Just remember, whatever reaction you have is the right one, okay? This is still the same year you buried your husband, the same cemetery. You don't have to be strong for Maddie. You can be whatever you want to be."

Kerry's jaw wobbled. "I know." She took a deep breath. "Let's just say, I've no idea what's going to happen once we're through those doors, because I've no idea what I'm thinking."

We got out and walked over to the main door, today

not being the kind of weather to stand outside. Overhead, the skies were grey, just like my heart. I hoped Maddie was okay. She was bearing up when I left her, it was Harris who was more of a mess. This was tough for both of them.

Inside, Gemma and Ally were already there, as were Rob and Jeremy, along with a smattering of Amos's friends. It wasn't a big gathering like James's funeral. But then, as you got older, I suspected your friendship groups splintered. Plus, Amos had worked abroad for much of his life as an engineer, so many of his friends had been unable to come. I knew Maddie had received plenty of cards and messages from them.

A tap on my shoulder made me turn, and I could see Kerry wondering who the person was. It was Lisa, Maddie's dad's ex, along with Maddie's half-brother, Nate. I gave them both a grateful hug.

Since Amos had died, Lisa had come around twice when I'd been there, and I could see why Maddie liked her. She was warm and compassionate, as was her son. While Lisa would never be Maddie's mum, I got the impression she was happy to fill a little of the void, and I know Maddie appreciated that. Perhaps, when Maddie got the nerve up to come around to my parents' house, my mum could fill a little more of it, too. Just as I thought that, Dean walked in, closely followed by Mum and Dad.

Something rose up in my throat when I saw them. Was I going to cry, finally? I steadied myself, ready for the onslaught of tears, but they didn't come. Dean and my parents walked up. I hugged my brother, then held on to Mum for far longer than necessary. That Maddie had buried her mum here suddenly took on far greater significance. No matter what happened in life, my parents had always been there for me. That was now in sharp focus.

"Thanks for coming," I whispered, barely able to get the words out, hugging Dad. "And for still being alive," I wanted to add, but didn't.

Mum stepped back, squeezing my arm. "You told me about it, and I know it's important. To you and to Maddie. So we all came."

We sat and waited for the main event, Kerry and I on the front bench, the irony not lost on me as I turned to smile at Gemma behind me. She mouthed the word "bench warmer" to me, and gave me a thumbs-up. I gulped. I was glad I was here for Maddie's uncle and not for Maddie. We were only just getting to know each other again, and I was not ready for that to come to an end.

The organ began and we stood. Before I knew it, the coffin was placed in front of us, and Maddie was beside me, her hand in mine, squeezing my fingers tight. On the other side, Kerry had hold of my other hand just as tight. My role here was to be the rock, the one everyone leaned on. I could totally do that, and was happy to do that. I wasn't going to cry, after all, so my hands may as well be useful.

But fuck me, I had no idea how Kerry was going to cope. Just being here was bringing back James's funeral in high definition. I looked to my left, where she was breathing out hard, trying to hold it together. To my right, Maddie was doing the same. They'd both endured so much grief, so much loss. I'd told both Kerry and Maddie to focus on the happy memories of their loved ones, but this was harder than even I'd thought. My breathing was getting scattered, but I had to be strong.

Kerry broke down when they played one of Amos's favourite songs — The Rolling Stones' 'You Can't Always Get What You Want' — which also happened to be one of James's. She broke in a silent way, her body heaving but no sound coming out. I heard movement behind, and then Gemma appeared next to Kerry, hugging her tight, comforting her. Emotion swirled inside me, the colours melting together like a stick of rock.

Then Maddie squeezed my hand again, clutching her speech cards. It was time for her eulogy. "You've got this," I whispered, before kissing her cheek.

She nodded, her eyes glistening.

I really hoped she did. We'd agreed that if she broke down, I'd get up and take over. Because of that, I knew the speech almost word for word.

When Maddie began to talk, Harris began to cry. I rubbed his arm, and his face crumpled. Maddie spoke about her exotic uncle working abroad, bringing them presents when he visited in their childhood. How he'd been there for her mum later in life. How much she loved him.

It was when she started talking about how much her mum loved Amos that I turned to my family behind.

I couldn't fathom saying goodbye to them. They were all here for me, my rocks, and I was so grateful. If I lost them, I wasn't sure what I'd do.

Suddenly, grief twisted itself like a knife in my gut, and I struggled to breathe. What was happening? Maddie's words about her family were swirling around my head like confetti, but I couldn't hear them. The sound of my own pain was too deafening, all the emotion I'd bottled up for the past ten years.

I stared at the coffin and saw James in my mind's eye. I turned to Kerry and thought of her unborn baby. I glanced at Maddie and saw our future, one that was impacted by death. I turned, just as Mum moved forward and kissed my cheek, giving my shoulder a squeeze.

That was all it took for the tears to start falling. Once they started, it seemed like they might never stop. I sat on the front bench as Harris took me in his arms, and listened to my love talk about her loss. And I grieved. For everything and everyone who'd gone. For Maddie's mum, Amos, for James, for the loss of us. It was horrific, but it was freeing.

Luckily, Maddie was a champion with the speech, which was a good job, because I would have been no use at all. When she sat down, she took my hand. I was semi-recovered, sitting upright, but the rest of the funeral passed by in a blur. When Amos disappeared behind the curtain, I cried again, just like everyone else.

I wasn't unusual anymore.

I was free.

At the end, Maddie and I embraced, as did she and her brother. Even though I was sodden with tears and grief, I felt lighter. Something had lifted from me. All the grief and upset I'd been storing had been let out into the world.

As I left our row, my parents were waiting for me, and I'd never been more grateful. I made a vow there and then never to take my parents for granted again.

I was even more grateful when Mum hugged Maddie first, and not me.

Chapter Thirty-Four

Dad had to leave for a job, but Mum came to the pub after the funeral. She stayed for two drinks and a slice of Gemma's chocolate orange cake, declaring it delicious and telling her she should open a cake school. Two glasses of wine and Mum thought she was a comedian. She headed off soon after, kissing me on the cheek and telling me she had a dental appointment. I pitied that dentist when she opened her mouth and breathed out a cloud of Chardonnay and sugar. She kissed us all goodbye, saving her longest hug for Maddie, telling her to come for dinner soon. That had me tearing up again, but dammit, I wasn't going to cry.

Maddie came and sat next to me afterwards, shaking her head. "Your mum's amazing, you know that?"

I smiled. "I do. She has her moments, today being an outstanding one."

"It was so great of both your parents to come. After how I treated you before, I was scared to see them. Especially your mum. But she told me in no uncertain terms I was always welcome in their home." She raised an eyebrow.

"Have you been bigging me up? She was glowing about how I'd helped you and Gemma."

I shook my head and glanced at my brother, who was chatting with one of Amos's friends. "Not me, you've got Dean to thank for that. He always did love you."

"Thank god for Dean." She leaned forward and kissed me. "And for you. Thanks for everything over the past few weeks, and the past few months. I seriously couldn't have done this without you, without everyone."

"Stop it, you're going to make me cry again." I shifted in my seat, still naked from my outpouring of emotion earlier. I'd already cried again at the wake when Maddie proposed a toast to her mum and uncle. Everyone was treating me with kid gloves, not quite sure what to make of the new Justine. If they were freaked, they should try being me.

"Fuck!"

I turned to see who was shouting obscenities at just gone 5pm, and fear ran up my spine when I saw Kerry doubled over, Dean's arm resting on her back. "Is she okay?" It was a stupid question, and not one I was proud of.

"No she's fucking not." Kerry always did have a way with words. She'd been complaining of feeling weird for the past hour or so, but we'd put it down to grief. But now? Maybe not.

"Are you in labour? Should I call an ambulance?"

"Yes you fucking should!"

Okay, Kerry was a sweary mother-to-be.

"And you're fucking coming with me, all of you." Kerry glanced up and looked around the table, all of whom had fallen silent.

I didn't think the ambulance would be happy taking all ten of us, but I glossed over that. "We're coming with you, don't worry." I glanced at Maddie, picking up my phone to go outside and call the ambulance. "Drink up, love. We're about to witness the miracle of birth, and the cycle of life. Birth and death in one day."

Chapter Thirty-Five

We left Kerry at the hospital in the capable hands of the staff and her family. Her sister was her birth partner, and her parents waited anxiously with us, giving us hugs at every opportunity. But Kerry's baby didn't take long to pop out: a boy, she named Stanley James after her late grandfather and her late husband. I liked that a baby named after two late family members was two weeks early.

We gave Kerry and Stanley our love, told her how proud James would have been, and I had one last sob when I held the baby. Then we jumped in a cab. I was just about to tell the cabbie Maddie's address, but she leaned forward and told the driver to take us to The Spanish Station. When she sat back on the black leather seat, I smiled at her.

"You always were a smoothie, you know that?"

"I try," Maddie replied.

When we got out, we strolled across the car park to the bar, hand in hand. I pulled my grey scarf a little closer around my neck as the October chill tried to bite through.

When we arrived, the place was half-empty, but the bar looked gorgeous. Twinkly lights were strung outside, along with fresh flowers. We ordered two glasses of wine, then sat outside under one of the outdoor heaters, looking out to the dockside, all lit up. It was still before 9:00 pm, but it felt like we'd been up for days. We'd packed a lifetime into the last 12 hours.

"So a funeral and a birth in one day. It's like we're inside a country song, isn't it?"

I laughed. "You could say that. You okay with Kerry upstaging Amos?"

"More than okay. I like that she let him have his time, then stole it at the last. It means that now when I think about today, it won't be tinged with quite as much sadness. Good things came out of it, too."

I put an arm around her and pulled her close. She let me.

"We had some good times here, didn't we?" Maddie said.

"We did."

"You think we can have some more good times?"

"It could be arranged."

"I've been thinking about the house. About what I want to do."

I turned to her. I'd been doing some thinking, too. "I know I've been putting pressure on you to stay in it, to put down some roots. But you know what? So long as you stay here and don't move away, you can live wherever you want. Wherever makes you happy. So long as we're together, that's the main thing. I don't want you to stay in that house if it has too many memories."

Maddie gave me a slow smile, a single eyebrow quirking. How I loved her no-nonsense brows. "Let me finish. What I was going to say before you interrupted me is that you were right."

"I was?" This was news.

"Uh-huh. That house holds a lot of memories, but most of them are good, not bad. Amos when he came to visit. Mum singing and cooking. Us having sex upstairs." She grinned, kissing my lips. "Plus, how can I move out when you love that kitchen so much?"

I leaned in to kiss her again. She tasted of my future.

Maddie stared into my eyes, still just inches from her own. "The point is, I've decided to stay put."

A warmth flooded my body like golden sunshine. I flung my arms around her neck and squeezed. "I'm so pleased." That was the understatement of the year.

She kissed me again. "I'm glad you're pleased. But I do have one condition."

I pulled back. "Condition?"

"Actually two. And they're big ones." She paused. "The first condition is that you move in with me. That's non-negotiable."

My heart burst like a firework in my chest, but I held it together. I could feel emotion wrapping itself around my tear ducts again, but I wasn't going to give in. Not just yet. Focus.

"The second condition is that we get a dog. A dachshund preferably, like I grew up with, but I'm open to suggestions. Just not a labrador. Too much phlegm."

"I never knew you were so picky with dogs."

"Every day's a school day." She paused, eyeing me closely. "So what do you think? Move in with me and get the kitchen of your dreams?"

"Are you blackmailing me?"

"In the nicest possible way. Plus, if your business is in Bristol, it makes sense, right? Think of all the traffic you'd avoid in the morning."

"That's the best reason yet."

Maddie's smile showed off her impossibly straight teeth. The straightest thing about her. "Is that a yes?"

"It's a big decision." I narrowed my eyes. I was trying to think of negatives, but I was coming up blank. These days, I could only see positives where Maddie was concerned.

"But you told me you were thinking of moving."

"I was. I am."

"So move in with me." Her eyes shone as she spoke.

"That would mean admitting you're my kind."

She moved as close as she could without kissing me. "I *am* your kind, in every possible way. Why wait anymore? We've waited a decade, and life's short. Let's grab it while we can, take a chance. Me, you, and our dog. I love you, Justine. I always have."

I gulped. So many times I'd dreamed of this moment, and now here it was. Maddie was back in my life, and she was asking me to move in with her. To trust her. To love her. I had to give it a chance. I had to go with my gut. My heart and my gut were screaming yes.

I nodded, relief surging through me. I'd found her again. Finally. "Yes. I'd love to move into your house with you. And we can have a dachshund." I paused. "I love you, too, by the way."

Maddie beamed and took me in her arms, holding me like she was never going to let me go.

I had to trust that was true. I had to trust in Maddie. I was determined to give it my best shot. Because wherever she was, I wanted to be.

In the end, it really was that simple.

Epilogue

One Year Later

"Something smells delicious!" I hung my scarf on the coat hook in the hallway and greeted Flash, our brown-and-black sausage dog who was barking at my feet. I walked through to the kitchen, putting the Victoria sponge I'd baked earlier on the counter-top. There before me was my girlfriend, cooking. She was doing it more and more often these days, even starting to enjoy it. Seeing as I'd been cooking all the meals since I'd moved in nine months ago, I was all for it. Even if she did leave the kitchen looking like a bomb had gone off.

I drew up behind her at the hob, got on tip-toes and nuzzled her neck through her hair. She squirmed as she always did, although being a few inches shorter, I could never get the purchase I wanted. I breathed her in, still loving her smell. Still loving her, more than ever, day by day.

"How's Diane's tagine today?" I pulled away, stepping over Flash before grabbing a glass from the cupboard.

278

Maddie had dug out her mum's old recipes and was going through them, one by one.

"Tasting great. I might be ready to move onto another recipe soon. I thought maybe Mum's apple pie next."

I glugged some water before replying. "I wholeheartedly approve of that."

"How was the class?" She put the cone-shaped lid on the pot and walked over, kissing me on the lips as Flash scurried around our feet. Maddie bent to pet him, before standing back up.

Today had been full-on: a class of 20 in studio A with Amisha and Jo; a class of 15 in studio B with Gemma. "Good. The studios are great, still new enough to love. Enquiries are going through the roof. So we're doing well. Plus, our new teachers are brilliant, which is a relief."

She spied the cake box. "And you brought cake?"

"Of course. Such a gorgeous meal needs an accompanying dessert. Even if I didn't make it." I gave her a grin. "Plus, my family would never forgive me. Mum and Dad, and Dean and Octavia are turning up in an hour."

Our 'Homes Under The Hammer' episode had been delayed and only aired last week. Dean was still smarting after he'd been cut out completely. It was a sore spot I intended to poke later, with the episode set up to watch again after dinner because my parents hadn't yet seen it. Maddie had told me I was being childish. I totally agreed, but it wasn't going to stop me.

I checked my watch. "Everything on course?"

She gave me a thumbs-up. "Ship-shape and Bristol fashion."

"Lucky we live in Bristol, then." I looked up through the skylight, the one that had drawn me back here, the one I'd always loved. The past nine months had gone by in a blur, and mostly had been the sweetest I'd ever tasted. Maddie had coped with the loss of her uncle well, going to grief counselling, which she'd never done with her mum. Crucially, she'd also talked to Kerry and I. Her response wasn't to run anymore. It was to slow down and see how she could alter her mood. That was a triumph of epic proportions and one that made me hopeful for our future.

"And you're feeling okay today? One year since Amos died." I glanced at the table, where I could still see him sitting sometimes. "It doesn't seem so long, does it?"

Maddie smiled at me. "It does and it doesn't. Sometimes I can feel him, and I was sure he was here with me today. Mum definitely was, telling me not to over-spice the tagine. She's so bossy."

I kissed her lips. "The apple doesn't fall far from the tree."

She was quiet for a moment, and then got some wine glasses from the cupboard, and a bottle of red from the rack. "I spoke to Kerry today, by the way. Stanley's walking already. She reckons he's a child genius and I didn't like to argue with her."

"He may well be, who knows?" I laughed. "Did she say how her date went the other night?"

Maddie nodded, giving me a glass. "Early days but she said he seemed nice. They're going out again next week, so who knows? Must be so weird dating again."

"Let's never have to do that again, okay?"

"Agreed." She popped the cork, poured wine into two glasses, and raised her own. "I don't want to dwell on this tonight, so let's have a toast now. To absent friends. To Mum, to Amos, to James. Wherever they are, thanks for making our lives better as long as you did."

I tapped my glass to hers.

"Could you check the front door's shut, by the way?" Maddie shivered. "I can feel a draught?"

I nodded and went into the hallway, but it all looked fine. I frowned, turning back. "The door's shut," I began. But the words dried in my throat as I walked back into the kitchen to find Maddie on one knee, her face flushed, a small ring box open in her hand. And inside, something sparkling. I put a hand to my chest, and the room swayed.

Oh fuck, was this really happening? Blood rushed to my cheeks and my face must have been a picture. I clutched one of the old dining chairs and swallowed hard. Maddie was proposing in this kitchen. It was too perfect.

Maddie gave me that smile she kept just for me, one solid eyebrow quirked as she looked up. "Justine Amelia Thomas, will you do me the honour of being my wife?"

A grin split my face as warmth washed down me. Then I was nodding. I wasn't good at quizzes, but I knew this answer straight away. This was me defying the universe, and defying the odds. I had a new home, a refreshed business, and soon, a new wife.

"Of course I fucking will," I replied.

Maddie was on her feet, and then I was in her arms, her embrace my favourite place.

In Maddie's old house, now *our* house, I was finally home.

THE END

Want more from me? Sign up to join my VIP Readers' Group and get a FREE lesbian romance, **It Had To Be You!** *Claim your free book here: www.clarelydon.co.uk/it-had-to-be-you*

Did you enjoy this book?

I hope you did! Whatever your answer, I wonder if you'd consider leaving me a review wherever you bought it. Just a line or two is fine, and could really make the difference for someone else when they're wondering whether or not to take a chance on me and my writing. If you enjoyed the book and tell them why, it's possible your words will make them click the buy button, too! Just hop on over to wherever you bought this book — Amazon, Apple Books, Kobo, Bella Books, Barnes & Noble or any of the other digital outlets — and say what's in your heart. I always appreciate honest reviews.

Thank you, you're the best.

Love,
Clare x

Also by Clare Lydon

Other Novels
The Long Weekend
Nothing To Lose: A Lesbian Romance
Twice In A Lifetime
Once Upon A Princess

London Romance Series
London Calling (Book 1)
This London Love (Book 2)
A Girl Called London (Book 3)
The London Of Us (Book 4)
London, Actually (Book 5)
Made In London (Book 6)

All I Want Series
All I Want For Christmas (Book 1)
All I Want For Valentine's (Book 2)
All I Want For Spring (Book 3)
All I Want For Summer (Book 4)
All I Want For Autumn (Book 5)
All I Want Forever (Book 6)

Boxsets
All I Want Series Boxset, Books 1-3
All I Want Series Boxset, Books 4-6
All I Want Series Boxset, Books 1-6
London Romance Series Boxset, Books 1-3

Printed in Great Britain
by Amazon